Three Guys Talking: When Ladies Fight Back

Three Guys Talking: When Ladies Fight Back

Book 2

Adeyinka O. Laiyemo, MD, MPH

DEDICATION

This novel is dedicated to those who strive to help others.

ACKNOWLEDGMENTS

To the glory of the Almighty, I say a heartfelt thank you to all of you from A to Z for your help and support. Also, a big shout out to my lady consultants, you know who you are.

FROM THE AUTHOR

Thank you for your interest in this second episode of the trilogy *Three Guys Talking*, a romantic seriocomic chronicle of the love life of Ray Marshall, Kamal Brown, and Adam Gray from their points of view.

They had discussed their problems in the first episode. Ray was lonely in his marriage, as his wife has largely ignored him and mainly attended to the needs of their children. Kamal's happy marriage to Bonita was being threatened by Kandie, his ex-wife, and mother of his only child, who was trying to win him back. Adam, then a forty-two-year-old widower, was in love with Nora, a twenty-one-year-old hottie who has been rejecting his love proposal while Aneida, then a thirty-nine-year-old divorcee who can be a mother for his two children, wanted them to tie the nuptial knot. The friends proffered solutions for one another. The plans were simple, direct, and practical. Unfortunately, human beings are too complicated.

Ray was supposed to woo Desiree, his wife of thirteen years, by being extra nice to her, assisting her with house chores, bonding better with his children, and losing some weight and exercising more in order to be physically fit. This was suggested to bring back the good old days and prevent his marriage from going off the cliff. This worked almost perfectly, but Desiree became pregnant again.

Adam did not feel choosing a wife should be this complicated. There should not be a big deal about him being in love with his now twenty-two-year-old soul mate. Unfortunately, her mother, who is his age mate, described him as "feverishly fighting furiously for a forbidden fantasy."

Kamal was poised to recruit Bonita as his bodyguard. This would be his temptation-preventing strategy against Kandie, who is determined to wrestle him away from Bonita. The problem was that there was no red line that Kandie was not prepared to cross to achieve her objective.

The stakes have only gotten higher, the challenges have only become more compounded, and the task ahead has only become more difficult for the three friends. Again, the three friends face difficult challenges and need to make important decisions. The situation of these three friends begs the emotional questions: should you be with the one you love or with the one who loves you? What then should happen if the one you love does not love you, and you don't love the one who loves you?

Contents

Prologue

The soccer ball was rolling downhill on the sand towards them. Kamal attempted to kick the ball back to the youngster who was running their way to retrieve the ball, but he missed. Ray went after the ball, stopped it with his right foot and kicked it, but the ball went a whopping sixty degrees away from the poor boy who was trying to retrieve his ball.

"You guys cannot make it in little league soccer," Adam remarked. "Honestly, I don't think you can make it in a miniature soccer league, either. Your aiming skills are so bad that if you were the ones piloting the Apollo mission to the moon, Neil Armstrong and his colleagues would have landed on Pluto instead."

"The ball was moving too fast downhill," Kamal gave his excuse for missing the ball and kicking air.

Ray did not bother to offer any explanation for his poor marksmanship. What he was discussing with his friends prior to the ball coming their way was more important. He would surely prefer to be a good marksman in aiming, targeting, and be successful in reaching Desiree's heart, his wife of fifteen years.

The three friends had met again at the Youth Development Follow-Up Conference in Maryland at the Gaylord National Resort and Convention Center. This magnificent edifice is located at the National Harbor in Oxon Hill, in close proximity to the District of Columbia and Virginia.

The four-hour conference had just ended, and the friends decided to take a stroll down the riverside of the National Harbor overlooking the well-decorated riverbanks of the Potomac River, across from Dyke Marsh Wildlife Preserve and Belle Haven marina.

Ray was eager to talk. He was anxious to brief his friends in terms of the interval developments since their discussions. "Since we last met and discussed, things have been going up and down between Desiree and me. Life has been a yo-yo," Ray remarked.

"My situation may be worse than yours then," Kamal opined. "It was as if I went from the frying pan into the fire. Kandie has become more vicious and virulent. She is a monster and has been persistently trying to create a wedge between Bonita and me," Kamal expressed regretfully.

As they walked by the sets of restaurants overlooking the Potomac River, they saw a branch of Heavenly Taste restaurant. Kamal looked at Ray with probing eyes.

"Is this a branch of that restaurant you mentioned that serves fantastic fries and salutary salmon for a million dollars?" Kamal asked.

"Yeah. It must be," Ray replied.

All of them quickened their steps. It was as if they did not want any curiosity to get them into entering the restaurant. They decided to enter *Pescado Delicioso*, a Mexican seafood restaurant. As they were ushered into their seats, Kamal observed that Adam did not say anything about what had transpired since they discussed.

"Don't tell me that you are still trying to suffer a self-inflicted heart attack from your twenty-year-old Nova," Kamal remarked in jest.

Adam snarled at Kamal. "First of all, her name is Nora, not Nova. Secondly, she is twenty-two now and will be twenty-three in a couple of months…"

"Thirdly," Kamal interjected, "you still want the headache and heart attack from her."

"Well, I met her family over dinner," Adam recalled.

"Really?" Kamal remarked with surprise. "You were invited to meet her family? Wow! How did it go?"

"Let's not talk about it," Adam replied.

"Absolutely not! We need to discuss this and know what happened. My friend, you may be the doctor, but when you eventually get that heart attack you are craving so much, you will need somebody else to give you CPR. There is a pretty good chance that I will be the one to give you the CPR." Kamal countered.

Ray looked at Adam with pouted lips and remarked, "It is a hardcore love, baby."

Kamal shook his head in disbelief. "Adam, you are the only guy I know who knows that heart attack is on the way and want to waylay it anyway. Have you forgotten that there is no easy solution for a broken heart?"

Avoid Broken Hearts
You cannot mend broken hearts
With needles and threads
You cannot fix broken hearts
With adhesives and glues
You cannot repair broken hearts
With hammers and nails
You cannot get rid of broken hearts
With stents and heart transplants
Avoid breaking people's hearts

It is apparent that the love lives of these friends are either complicatedly simple, or simply complicated. Everything has been about the choices they made and the choices that they are still going to make.

The Perils of Choice
Our first choice
May not be our best choice
Our preferred choice
May not be our sensible choice

Part One

Moving forward:
The story of Ray

Part One: Section One:
Back on track

Ray was jolted back to reality by the driver behind him who blew his car horn to a deafening degree to alert Ray that the light had turned green. This occurred at the intersection leading to Alexandria Mall, a mega-complex in Fairfax County. This was his first time in this mall since he and his family moved from Silver Spring to Fort Washington. The light just turned green for the left turn at the busy Richmond Highway entrance into the complex. The driver behind him was obviously in a hurry, as the light had barely changed color from red to green for more than a second. Ray wondered if the driver just wanted to prove that the horn in his vehicle works. In that case, he should simply take his vehicle for Virginia State inspection, and he can blow his stupid horn as much as he wants during the test.

"What exactly is he in a hurry to go and buy anyway that is making him so impatient?" Ray asked himself.

Ray had been lost in thought briefly but snapped back to reality now as he made his way into the parking lot in front of *The Exquisite*, a popular clothing store in the mall. He was a little bit apprehensive of his mission. The last time he was in a clothing store by himself to buy clothes was about eight years ago. He could not even remember what he bought. Desiree had been the one who has been buying clothes for him. Today, he came to the mall to buy some clothes for himself. He mused as he thought about how Desiree has surely spoiled him. Then he quickly "corrected himself" because as a matter of fact, he was the one who spoiled Desiree by allowing her to buy clothes for him to wear. He chuckled at his reasoning, recognizing that he was lying to himself. The last time he was in any clothing store was four years previously. He was dragged there by Desiree who accompanied him and literarily arm-twisted him to buy a tuxedo for an important formal luncheon. He seized the opportunity to buy some suits as well.

This additional task for Desiree was brought about by her persistent complaint to Ray to change some of his clothes, but he never did. It all reached a climax one Friday morning when Ray was dressing up to leave for work.

"Please, Ray, not that blue shirt again," Desiree pleaded.

"What is wrong with it? It is perfectly fine." Ray replied.

"Everything is wrong with it, Ray. You have been wearing these clothes since undergrad."

"Absolutely not!"

"Okay, since law school."

"No!" Ray responded shaking his head.

"Yes!" Desiree affirmed nodding her head.

"Of course not! I only wore large shirts in law school. This is extra-large."

He walked towards Desiree in order to show her the label of the shirt, and he remarked, "It is my lucky shirt."

"Were you wearing it when we met?" Desiree asked sarcastically.

"Of course not! We met when I was in law school. Remember?" Ray replied.

"Then, there is nothing 'lucky' about this old shirt," Desiree responded, making air quotes on mentioning the word lucky.

"Well, I bought it after we got married," Ray explained.

"But we got married six years, three children, and another one on-the-way ago," Desiree reminded him pointing to her protuberant abdomen, as she was seven months pregnant.

Ray simply shook his head, but Desiree came closer to him and snatched the shirt from him.

"Look at it!" She pointed at the collar with her right

fingers while holding the shirt with her left. "Even the collar has changed from blue to something else."

"Lighter blue?" Ray replied chuckling. "Maybe it is the detergent that you are using to wash the clothes that you need to change!"

"It is not funny!" Desiree remarked.

"I am convinced that either the washer or the detergent you are using changed the color a bit," Ray concluded.

Desiree did not bother to reply to this unwarranted accusation. That day, Ray wore a different shirt to work but did not buy any new clothes. Three weeks later, Desiree was completely frustrated. Despite her advanced pregnancy and her challenges with their three small children who could almost pass for triplets, she went to a men's clothing store and bought clothes for Ray. When she got back home, Ray was watching TV. He was engrossed watching the Bowl Championship Series. The Feeding Fiesta Bowl football game was between The Loving Gamecocks of the University of Central Carolina and the Fighting Green Hens of the University of Central Delaware. He thought the names of the mascots were intriguing but true. In his opinion, males are loving creatures, and that is why they always go to the females. However, females are always fighting, and that is why they chase men away. He mused to himself at this thought even though he knew that it was not completely true. The football game was not even close. The Hens took it to the Gamecocks and ran the ball 'down their throats' with an unrelenting authority. The Hens had forty points, while the Gamecocks were only able to manage two field goals for a total of six points. It was five minutes to the end of the game when Desiree came back with shopping bags and gave the clothes to Ray for him to try them on. After some weakly spirited arguments from Ray claiming that he did not need the clothes, he finally agreed to try them on but only after the game. About fifteen minutes later, the game was over with the Gamecocks scoring a meaningless touchdown as time expired. The Hens won by a final score of forty to thirteen points and were given the trophy.

Ray looked inside the shopping bags and saw that

Desiree had bought him shirts, pants, undershirts, and boxers. He shook his head, saying to himself, "Women. You can't live with them, and you can't live without them."

When Desiree saw that Ray had finally gotten up from the couch where he had been wasting time doing nothing useful for about three hours, watching a stupid football game, she shook her head saying to herself, "Men. You can't put up with them, and you can't put them down."

When the children saw that daddy has finally put down the remote control of the television, meaning that they can now watch their favorite cartoon programs, they said to themselves, "Parents. You want to love them, and you want to leave them."

"So, did she get your size and fittings, right?" Adam inquired from Ray.

"Oh, yes. She was pin-point accurate with her choices. I doubt if I could have made better choices myself," Ray reflected.

"And then what happened?" Kamal asked.

"Nothing." Ray responded.

"You did not even say *thank you* to her for going to buy you clothes while dragging three small children to the store and being seven months pregnant?" Kamal asked with a bewildered look on his face.

"Unfortunately, I did not. Remember that I was young and stupid back then," Ray explained.

"You are probably still stupid but no longer young," Adam opined.

"I am a much better person now, believe me. The worse part was that I actually protested that she went to buy the clothes," Ray explained.

"So, what boneheaded thing did you do?" Kamal asked.

"I wore the rest of the clothes, but I refused to wear the underwear for one week," Ray recalled.

"So, what made you change your mind?" Kamal inquired.

"I ran out of underwear. The only ones I could find that day were the new ones she bought."

Kamal and Adam looked at each other and nodded. They

knew that Desiree took all the underwear away out of frustration, but they did not need to tell Ray about that.

Ray continued. "These days, I realized that my clothes just disappear like those anti-government opposition party members in developing countries during an election year."

"Is that what happened to your lucky blue shirt?" Kamal asked in jest.

"Come to think about it, you are right. I do not believe that I ever saw it after that encounter with Desiree."

"In essence, Desiree has been buying clothes for you for many years now," Adam confirmed.

"That is true. The only thing was that I later told her that I preferred pleated front pants over flat fronts. The flat front pants make my thighs look fat," Ray explained.

"Yeah right," Adam remarked while chuckling. "Your statement is reminiscent of the popular question purportedly often asked by ladies, "Do these clothes make me look fat?""

"So, how do you answer that?" Ray asked with keen interest.

"It is a no-look answer...absolutely not!" Adam responded.

"What do you mean by no-look?" Ray asked.

"I hope you never get that question. However, if you do, you do not need to look at the lady who asked you to answer that question. In the first place, you are never going to tell her that she is fat. Secondly, she did not ask you if she is fat. If she is, she knows that already. The question was whether her clothes were giving the impression that she is fat. Clothes don't make people fat. People are either fat or not depending on their body size. So, you do not need to look at the lady before reassuring her that her clothes are not making her look fat," Adam concluded.

"I get your point," Ray admitted. He then continued. "After our discussion, I had to go to the store to buy some sportswear and running shoes for my exercise regimen that you guys suggested. When I got to the front of the store, I had a major decision to make: To take a cart or not to take a cart? That was the question. I figured that if I did not take a cart, I would limit myself to buying only things that I needed in the mall. However, if I have a cart in my possession, I may buy more things than I intended. On the other hand, if I bought a lot of stuff, carrying them by hand would be difficult. It took me about five minutes to decide to take a cart."

Ray looked at his friends and remarked, "You see how much in-depth analysis I do now, and I am very patient while making decisions these days, unlike the day I met Desiree in college."

Adam and Kamal nodded in agreement, and Kamal remarked, "Old age has its perks."

Ray continued. "When I got to the sportswear section for men, I noticed that they have many varieties of apparel. As I was trying to analyze which ones to buy, a guy standing across from me offered a piece of unsolicited advice."

"What did he say?" Kamal inquired.

"He told me to buy a moisture-wicking fabric so that it does not stick to me after a long sweaty workout. I looked up to see this huge and very muscular gym rat. I felt he deliberately wore tight-fitting clothes to show off his pecs and guns. He asked me what type of exercises I plan to be doing, and I told him any exercises that would improve my strength and cardio endurance. He later told me that his name is David. Honestly, given his size, his name should have been Goliath. Anyway, he informed me that he is a personal fitness trainer at a local gym called Diamond Fitness about a mile away and recommended that I come there. Later, I went to the shoe section, and I was assisted by a female attendant there who scientifically picked a pair of running shoes for me."

"What did you mean that she 'scientifically' picked running shoes for you?" Adam inquired, making air quotes on mentioning scientifically.

"I was surprised too. She asked me what type of running shoes I was looking for. I replied that I wanted something comfortable enough for me to run a marathon." Ray recalled.

"You ran a marathon?" Adam exclaimed, being very surprised.

"Yes, I eventually did. However, at the time I was talking

to the attendant, I was only joking. I mean it was like…like a figure of speech," Ray explained.

"Impressive!" Adam remarked.

"Congratulations, brother!" Kamal commented while shaking Ray's hands. "You have accomplished what most human beings will not."

Ray thanked his friends with a smile of accomplishment streaming across his face. He then continued his narration. "The shoe section attendant asked me to walk so that she could see my walking pattern to determine the best match for me while taking my arch support needs and gait into consideration."

"Really?" Adam remarked, being surprised.

"I was surprised too. I have never been asked by a lady to walk for her to observe me before. Usually, and I mean when I was much younger, when a lady asked me to *take a walk*, it generally meant that I was bothering her, and she wanted me to *go away!*" Ray recalled.

Kamal and Adam burst into uncontrollable laughter.

"Seriously," Ray continued, "I got a lot of that from my sisters when we were growing up."

"Of course, I can easily imagine that…knowing how annoying you can be," Adam opined.

"Anyway, I did as I was told, but it felt creepy. I felt as if I was being watched and judged. I did not know what to make of it. At that moment, I wondered how ladies feel when they are walking and going about their business and thirsty guys keep starring at them," Ray wondered.

"I am sure it must make them feel uncomfortable too," Kamal reasoned.

"But ladies may actually enjoy that attention they get when guys are looking at them and admiring them," Adam suggested.

"That may be applicable to those who are in fashion shows to display new designer clothes. I think that is why they actually catwalk to get maximum attention. I am guessing that the guys who attend those displays are actually looking at the ladies rather than the design of the clothes they are wearing," Kamal opined.

"On a curious note, I know that ladies hate catcalls because it is nothing but harassment. However, do ladies really like when guys are looking at them or as some people say, *checking them out,* even if they are not saying anything?" Adam wondered.

Kamal and Ray shrugged their shoulders, indicating that they don't know.

> **Author's note:** Do ladies like guys to "check them out" even if they do not say anything? Is it true that most ladies feel that guys are typically staring at their cleavages when they talk to them directly without lowering their gaze? Do ladies prefer guys not to look at them directly when they talk to them?

Ray continued. "After walking a short distance in the shoe aisle, the attendant asked me to walk back. Then she analyzed my walking pattern, described my arch, measured my feet, and later came back with two different running shoes for me to try. I ended up paying about a hundred and twenty bucks for just a pair of running shoes. It was a bit expensive, but after all the "scientific concierge" service in picking a running shoe, I guess that I felt it was well worth it. I later went to the fitting room to try on the sportswear that I picked."

Ray took a sip of his drink and continued. "When I got to the fitting room section, the attendant asked me how many clothes I planned to try on, and I told her fourteen."

"Fourteen?" Adam and Kamal asked in unison.

"Yeah. Seven shirts and seven pants," Ray replied. "I figured that I would be exercising every day. In any case, the attendant informed me that the store policy was that a customer can only go into the fitting room with a maximum of six items of clothing. So, I ended up trying them in batches. I bought all the fourteen shirts and pants, the running shoes, and some athletic socks."

"You were highly motivated. So, did you hit the gym right away?" Kamal inquired.

"Of course not! I left all the clothes on their hangers in

my closet for two months without wearing any of them." Ray recalled.

The three of them burst into laughter.

"So, what made you change your mind since you mentioned earlier that you ran in the Marine Corps Marathon in Washington DC?" Kamal inquired.

"Yeah. How did you then get back to exercising? I am pretty sure that it is impossible to get off the couch and run a marathon and still be alive?" Adam expressed.

"Desiree got on my nerves," Ray replied.

"What happened?" Adam asked Ray.

"One Saturday, while we were arguing about something which I do not remember, the conversation turned ugly, and Desiree became raving mad. I did not care. All of a sudden, she looked at me and called me a hypocrite."

"Hypocrite?" Adam sought clarification.

"Yes. She called me a hypocrite. She said that I often looked at her and passed some unsalutary comments about how she looked, forgetting that she gave birth to four children within six years for me. She made it sound as if she did me a favor. She then shouted, "Look at you! You look like you are ten months pregnant!""

Kamal and Adam looked at each other and tried not to laugh. After a few seconds, Kamal asked, "On a curious note, how did you reply?"

"I don't know. All I remembered was yelling at her in a soft voice, and she yelled back in a loud voice. Thereafter, I went into the bedroom and slammed the door."

After spending some time in the bedroom without doing anything in particular, Ray recalled that he looked at Desiree's dresser and mirror in the bedroom. The dresser was made with solid cherry wood. It has multiple drawers with easy pull metal glides. She also has an additional standing mirror which is Cappuccino in color. It has a smooth and simple frame with a sophisticated look. The mirror is about 42 inches long, and it is front-facing with four angle tilting design. Her makeup and those feminine things in little bottles and flat containers caught his attention in the drawer, and he examined some of them.

"Did you guys know that lipsticks have expiry dates?" Ray asked.

"Really?" Adam queried looking puzzled.

"Yes, they do. Many of those feminine products have *best-by* dates on them. I was surprised too." Ray related.

"I mean...em...em...these are waxes and colorings, right? Why would they expire?" Adam expressed surprise.

"Well, they do. I guess it is part of the global conspiracy of women against men to make sure that we are always spending money. In general, eye and lip pencils can last for about five years while eye shadows and lipsticks last for about two years, but mascara only lasts for about six months. Anyway, I noticed that a lot of that makeup stuff belonging to Desiree has actually expired. It made me wonder why she didn't use them before they expired. I know women are very complicated. For example, they will shave their eyebrows and then use a marker to paint it back to the same spot. I mean, how does that make any sense? Why wouldn't they just use the marker over the eyebrows directly if they wanted them darker? That said, I was shocked to see that she bought this stuff and did not use them. Just a blatant waste of money! I guess that getting married was her goal, sustaining the flame of her husband's love was not her priority," Ray rationalized.

"C'mon! My friend, I am sure you understand why she called you a hypocrite," Kamal surmised. "She felt that you were criticizing her that she was letting herself go instead of making efforts to remain attractive to you, but she felt that you were doing the same. Let's face it. You bought gym clothes and running shoes without using them too."

"Well, she is entitled to her wrong opinion. Anyway, when I looked in the mirror, I saw a very handsome young man..."

"Was there a picture on the wall behind you?" Kamal asked, interrupting Ray.

"No, why do you ask?" Ray responded.

"Because the person you just described did not match you!" Kamal replied, laughing.

"Kamal, you are not serious!" Ray replied and faced

Adam. "I did my own version of posing at Mr. Olympia competition with my shirt on. Then, I took off my shirt to see my big muscles directly. I contracted my biceps standing at an angle to the mirror and shouted, yeah, baby!"

Adam and Kamal looked at each other and chuckled.

Ray ignored them and continued. "Then, I looked at my six-packs..."

"Did you find them?" Kamal asked sarcastically interjecting Ray.

"Of course. They are not lost. They just needed a systematic way of looking...em...em...for you to see them."

"So, how long did it take you to find them?" Kamal asked in jest.

"Only about ten minutes," Ray responded while trying hard to maintain a straight face.

"Were they arranged vertically and horizontally like a crossword puzzle, since they were playing hide and seek with you?" Adam inquired while laughing.

At this point, the three of them burst into laughter.

Ray continued, "I also tried contracting my pecs, but they did not move."

"I guess they were caught up in the hide and seek game with your six packs too, or they were simply protesting," Adam offered an explanation with tongue in cheek.

"I am going to punch you," Ray threatened jokingly. "Well, I then turned to my side and looked at the contour of my abs. Men! Desiree was exaggerating. She was absolutely lying. I did not look ten months pregnant at all."

"Maybe six months?" Adam suggested.

"Absolutely not. At most, maybe three months," Ray estimated.

"C'mon Ray! Three months pregnancy is not really noticeable because the uterus is typically still in the pelvis or probably just making its way out into the abdomen proper," Adam countered.

"In any case, I am not pregnant. Remember that if we paraphrase the famous quote from George Orwell's *Animal Farm*, we will agree that *all men have six-packs, some six-packs are just more visible than others*. My six-pack just needed some exercise. So, I went to the basement, opened the closet and brought out our treadmill and two free weights: one was twenty pounds, and the other was thirty pounds. I had bought them with the treadmill from Sports Cave many years previously. I plugged in the treadmill, and that baby worked!" Ray exclaimed with joy.

Adam and Kamal looked at each other and smiled.

Ray continued, "I lifted those weights a few times and ran on the treadmill for about thirty minutes using the programmed workout schedule on the equipment. Unfortunately, the motivation for the exercise did not last at all. After three days, I stopped exercising again."

"How did you then get back to exercising? I am pretty sure that you didn't get off the couch to run a marathon," Adam expressed.

"Well, you are right. About a week later, when we were in a relaxed mood on the couch, Desiree asked me why I stopped using the treadmill in the basement. I replied that the exercise was no fun at all. I told her that I prefer the exercise that we do together between the sheets. This made her shake her head with a smile and she quickly walked away. Actually, she ran away!"

The three friends burst into laughter.

Ray continued. "A few minutes later, I decided to go to the basement and give exercising another try. To my surprise, Desiree came to join me. It was the best exercise moment ever! I mean...the second best exercise type...em...em...exercise moment ever! You understand what I mean!"

Adam and Kamal chuckled. "Yes, we understand," they replied almost in unison.

Ray continued. "It was the beginning of a new era for us...sort of. We started having something to do together that does not involve us yelling at each other. We got to just talk. Sometimes, we did more talking than exercising. I started getting more informed and more involved in what I called "The home affairs." A lot of the time, when I get home from work, I would ask her if she needed me to do anything. Sometimes there was, but a lot of time, there was nothing she needed me to do. Although she still said her annoying *"no, leave me alone", "I have a headache"* rejections, the frequency went down somewhat. Maybe it was my expectation that went down, who knows? Nonetheless, our relationship improved."

"That's good!" Kamal exclaimed

"Well, that is true. However, what I realized was that her rejections of us traveling to the land of pleasure together had little or nothing to do with how much work she did."

"Really? I don't understand what you mean" Kamal expressed.

"It was not about how much work she did when I was away at work; it was more about her mindset about how important her comfort duty to me is! For example, she could have worked all day and be visibly tired, but she wouldn't say no. Rather, she may actually be looking forward to it as a relaxation intervention. On the other hand, she may have little or nothing to do, and she will still pester me with her unjustifiable *leave me alone*. In my opinion, I think that understanding that it is a duty or responsibility, whatever we want to call it, is the key. That said, a very cordial relationship will help make such duties easier to perform." Ray explained.

Better together

How I feel about you
Is very hard for me to explain
Why I long so much for you
Is impossible for me to ascertain
What I can achieve with you
Is far beyond what I can solely attain
Whenever I talk to you
Is a period of joy that I want to retain
When I am with you
Is happiness that I want again and again
Where I want to end up with you
Is the special place of supreme gain

Now that I know
What my life will be with you

I don't want to know
What my life will be without you

Let us go together
Let us be together
Let us work together
We are better together

I love you!

Suddenly there was an uproar in the restaurant. The three friends looked up at the television screen near their table and realized that Mexico had just scored a goal against Argentina in a soccer match. It was scored by the Captain of the team, a perfect header into the top right corner of the goal post from a free kick.

Part One: Section Two:
Keep moving

"Anyway, our relationship improved. I got a lot more involved with issues affecting the kids. We even took a trip to Philadelphia to see the Liberty Bell." Ray continued.

"That's nice," Adam remarked.

"I almost canceled the trip out of frustration. I probably would have regretted it if not for a measured dose of patience on my part at the right time." Ray related feeling proud of his achievement.

Adam looked at Kamal and remarked, "You better help this dude from developing back pain from patting himself on the back."

Kamal responded jokingly while facing Ray, "Hey dude! Stop patting yourself on the back so hard. We may have to call Desiree to get the truth from her."

Ray replied with fake perky laughter. "Please go ahead and call her. You can reach her on her favorite cellphone number: 1-800- *no no no, please leave me alone!*"

Before Adam and Kamal could react to his fake phone number, Ray remarked "I am so sorry, I think I messed up the number. It is actually 1-888-*no no no leave me alone please!*"

Kamal shook his head and remarked, "You really need help!"

"I concur!" Adam exclaimed.

Ray simply ignored them and continued, "As I was

saying before I was rudely and crudely interrupted by two no-good amigos, it was the first time my family had ever taken a road trip vacation anywhere. It was quite accidental, though. I think Paige had social studies homework about The United States Declaration of Independence, and we had a booklet of forever stamps with the Liberty Bell on it. There were some conversations about it, and an argument ensued about how big it is. So, I casually remarked that since it is only about three hours away, we could just go and see it. Somehow, Bryan became very ecstatic about the idea and shouted *yay*!. He ran quickly to inform Patricia that "daddy is taking us to ring the Liberty Bell," All of a sudden, they were all looking forward to it. So, it became a mission, and it sounded like a great idea."

"So, it was a spur of the moment decision?" Adam asked.

"True, but those kinds of things are the memories that children often have of their childhood that helps erase other bad stuff they witnessed growing up. You know, memorable things that their family did together." Ray surmised. "I suggested to Desiree that over that weekend, maybe we should take a weekend getaway trip to the city of brotherly love. She thought it was a great idea too. So, I booked a hotel for Friday and Saturday nights so that we can return by Sunday afternoon. That way, we would pause our typical 'rat race' life. I came home early on Friday hoping that we could be on our way around four p.m. so that we could get to our destination hotel suite by seven p.m. I had packed my bag the day before. When I got home, it was a disaster. It was as if a tornado landed in the house. Everything was in disarray. The worst part was that they were not ready for us to leave at all, and I really did not want us to drive when it was too dark. I became furious and yelled at Desiree in a soft voice, complaining about her poor timing. She did not respond."

"Of course, you only yell in a soft voice!" Kamal remarked.

"While I was walking around the house complaining bitterly with my anger on full display, I accidentally stepped on one of those tiny plastic action figures belonging to Bryan. I think it was The Punisher or The Iron Man. It was very painful, as if I had stepped on a nail. It made me angrier. I wished we could just talk to the director of NASA and put all these kids in a space shuttle and send them to Mars or Jupiter. With a painful foot, I decided to just calm down. So, I put on the television to watch some game highlights on ESPN. After about five minutes, I felt Desiree's hand on my right shoulder, and she whispered calmly in my left ear, "You do know that we will be faster if you actually help." There was something disarming about the way she said it, and it jolted me into the reality that she was actually correct. Yelling at her or getting angry with the children is never going to solve the problem but compound it. I tell you guys, if she had always talked to me like that, we would probably never fight."

Kamal and Adam looked at each other and shook their heads. Kamal then remarked, "you may still fight. However, it will be a lot fewer and would not drag on for too long especially if your screws aren't too loose."

I switched off the television and got involved in helping the kids and Desiree do whatever needed to be done. Honestly, the kids straightened up, the bickering stopped, and within thirty minutes we were ready to leave. We took the mid-size sports utility vehicle so that we would have enough space to fit all of us and our baggage. I realized that the vehicle had accrued a lot of miles, even from the last oil change. It really gave me a pause, and I contemplated how much driving Desiree does and the incredible effort it actually takes to raise children. I took Desiree's left hand and lovingly squeezed the back of her hand. She looked at me and asked, "What?" I replied, saying "Nothing! I just think we make a great team." This made her shake her head, and I could see that beautiful smile streaming across her face. In actual fact, saying *thank you* to her for all her efforts and sacrifice would have been better.

**Whoever says homemaker mums stay at home has
no idea what he or she is talking about!**

"It actually helps to help. Unfortunately, as simple as it sounds, most men don't actually know to do so," Kamal regretted.

"As I was finally pulling out of the driveway, Lisa started crying. She said that she forgot Teddy, her teddy bear. It was as if my head would explode. So, I said, "Too bad," and continued reversing the car. Desiree then addressed me calmly and said, "Darling, please let us get it for her. It will only make things easier for her and us." Guys, I am not sure where Desiree found this patience. I found it irresistible to say no to her requests. It was as if she had been meditating and had this inner peace of some sort. I mean, rather than being furious or argue with her, I calmly got out of the car and I went to get the teddy bear."

"I guess patience and kind words can soften even a heart of stone like yours," Kamal surmised.

"My heart is softer than a jellyfish. Yours, on the other hand, is harder than a diamond," Ray retorted.

"No. My heart is more precious than a diamond, softer than talc, whiter than snow, and sweeter than honey," Kamal opined.

"Don't mind him, Ray, he is full of it," Adam chimed in.

"Well, at least it is obvious that I have a heart," Kamal responded.

"And you think that I don't?" Adam queried.

"At least it is not in your chest! I think it is with Nova, who is busy crushing it," Kamal reasoned.

"You are not serious!" Adam replied. "Moreover, her name is Nora, not Nova. I think you are having early dementia, or did you forget to take your medicine? Never mind, my apologies. Dementia will make you forget to take your medicine. So, it is a revolving door of misery."

Kamal simply shook his head and did not respond.

Ray continued his story, "The drive to Philadelphia was uneventful. The annoying *are we there yet?* questions stopped shortly after sunset since the children and Desiree fell asleep. I started recalling all the events that happened in the house shortly before we left. I contemplated on how annoying the children were and how frustrating it was to get everybody out of the house. Then I asked myself a provocative question. If there was a situation and I could only take a child with me, who will I take? In essence, who is my favorite child?"

"I only have one child, so I may not be qualified to answer such a question. However, I don't think that a parent can actually pick a favorite child. Wouldn't they love all of them equally?" Kamal wondered.

"I don't think you can love two people equally, regardless of your relationship with them. It is a matter of the heart and emotions. It is very hard to predict." Adam opined.

Ray continued, "Since I had nothing to do other than to focus on my driving on I-95 North. I continued to analyze the question. I almost quickly concluded that it would be one of the girls because women generally take better care of their parents. Men are generally taken away by their wives. In my opinion, this is why it is ridiculous and foolish to prefer boys over girls as children. In comparing Patricia with Lisa, I initially thought that I would probably prefer Patricia because she is older and will be independent sooner and I can sigh relief that she will be gone with her husband soon."

"Really?" Kamal remarked. "You made it sound as if you chose her to get rid of her."

"Not exactly, but a bird has got to leave the nest someday," Ray replied.

"You are really crazy," Kamal opined.

Ray simply ignored him and continued. "Somehow, I just couldn't see how I could pick her over Lisa, my darling little girl. Lisa is the only one who is still excited to see me when I get home. She will always come to the door to hug me when I get home. That feeling is priceless. Then, it occurred to me that girls tend to move away from daddy when they become teenagers because they think daddies are in this world to embarrass them and to chase boys away. They only come to daddy smiling when they want to *borrow* your credit card when going to the mall. Boys, on the other hand, tend to be low maintenance. It is easier to find common ground with them and establish a bond of friendship, at least until their wives take them away forever. I realized that I wanted an enduring father-child relationship. In the end, it was impossible to pick my favorite child."

"Interesting analysis!" Adam remarked.

Ray continued, "The greatest challenge with taking a family trip…is taking the family on a trip. This is because there are just too many moving parts." Nonetheless, the trip to Philadelphia was awesome. We ordered dinner from a drive-through on our way to Philadelphia, and we just crashed into the bed after checking into the hotel. Indeed, it was a great night.

<u>A Great Night</u>
It was a quiet night
It was a happy night
It was a blissful night
It was a peaceful night

It was a caring night
It was a relaxing night
It was a rewarding night
It was a fulfilling night

It was an affectionate night
It was a passionate night
It was a compassionate night
It was a blessed night

A night of sweet surrender
A night to fondly remember
A night that will last forever
A night to savor forever and ever

Even though this was merely a weekend getaway and involved staying only two nights in the hotel, it took quite some logistics. I did due diligence in booking the hotel to be close to downtown Philadelphia, and I planned some activities for us while we were there. I booked a hotel with breakfast to reduce the challenges of having to look for food in the mornings.

On Saturday morning, not surprisingly, we woke up late and hurriedly freshened up to get the complimentary hot breakfast in the hotel's breakfast section. It was a good value for money and was indeed a five-star breakfast. The breakfast menu was self-service with scrambled eggs, boiled eggs, French toast, different types of bagels, cold cereal, steaming hot oatmeal, and grits. They even had waffles made to order by one of the service personnel. It was outstanding. Later, we dressed up and went to those historic places downtown. We went to Independence Hall, where the Declaration of Independence was adopted and the United States Constitution was written. We also went to the Liberty Bell pavilion. They did not allow us to touch the bell. So, there was no ringing the Liberty bell by the kids. Of course, I expected that they would not let us ring it, especially given the fact that it cracked when it was rung the first time many centuries ago. Later, we drove to the Philadelphia Museum of Arts. The excursion was not easy because it involved a lot of walking with children, but it was well worth it. In the evening, we just stayed in the hotel watching television. The amazing thing was that the hotel suite has adjoining rooms and two televisions. So, the boys and I watched College

Football while the girls and their mum watched…whatever they watched. We stayed awake just relaxing till very late in the night with everybody sleeping wherever they slept overnight. We checked out of the hotel just before noon and headed back home, enduring a lot of traffic on I-95 on our way back. Nevertheless, it was a weekend to remember. It highlighted a simple and relatively inexpensive thing that we could do together as a family to promote bonding," Ray concluded.

Give me liberty or give me a great lover!

"The trip to Philadelphia was a big ray of hope for Desiree and me. If I had known that just leaving the house for a weekend can increase our bonding like that, I would have done it many times. It was a fresh breeze of life. It felt like a new beginning. I had found gold at the end of my own personal rainbow. When we got home, I went to the store to buy something Desiree told me we needed, and I saw a beautiful card with a picture of a rainbow on it. The cover message simply said, "HOPE." I bought the blank card and wrote a message to Desiree from my heart."

My rainbow
It is wonderful
Just like you
It is beautiful
Just like you
It is colorful
Just like you
It makes me hopeful
Just like you

You made me see the rainbow
You made me feel the rainbow
You made me touch the rainbow
You made me taste the rainbow
You made me blend with the rainbow

Thank you for coming to my life
Thank you for being my wife
Thank you for being the joy of my life
Thank you for being my rainbow

I love you

Ray continued, "After we returned home, our relationship improved. I showed her that I really care about her feelings."

"And how did you do that?" Adam inquired.

"I made sure that I ask her how she is and if she needed

me to do anything. I did it very frequently, almost every day," Ray replied.

"That is very nice of you. However, you should have been doing that a long time ago. You are a really slow learner," Kamal remarked.

"It seems that you really have problems with giving encouraging words. Are you sure that you are not lying that Desiree did not pay you to always take her side?" Ray questioned.

"Thank you for bringing it up. As a matter of fact, you owe me a thousand dollars in unpaid bills from my services to Desiree. I take cash and *major* credit cards," Kamal replied.

"Poor you! Unfortunately, I only brought my *minor* credit card today. I have some check leaflets though. My *major* credit card is with Desiree. She is using it to buy things for her kids," Ray replied.

"*Her* kids? Here you go again. *Her* kids?" Kamal questioned raising his voice.

Adam looked at Kamal and remarked, "Cut the brother a slack. You know that he is just joking. In any case, please stop interrupting him,"

Ray looked at Adam and remarked. "Thank you. One of these days, I am going to ask you to beat him up on my behalf. As I was saying, Desiree and I tried to have our exercise nights four times a week. Unfortunately, the children's issues sometimes got in the way. Those school projects always come at the wrong time! What can we do? We kept trying our best. I also tried to help the children with their homework as much as I could. Unfortunately, this feel-good period did not last long. After some time, Desiree kept saying "no" so frequently to the point that I started feeling ashamed to ask. To keep my sanity, I decided to go to Diamond Gym and joined as a member. I was going irregularly at first, not fully utilizing the money I paid. As I got more and more discontented at home, I started working out more, but it was a disaster.

"Why? What happened?" Adam inquired.

"My friend, when people tell you that you should

exercise to burn off calories so that you do not have too much energy for the best exercise known to man, they really don't know what they are talking about," Ray opined.

"I am not sure that I understand what you mean," Adam reiterated.

"Remember when I told you guys that we went to seek counseling from Dr. Nit Wit and she recommended that I go join a gym and burn calories every night so that I do not have too much energy and I can stop bothering my exhausted housewife?" Ray asked.

"Yes, I remember," Kamal responded.

"Well, she is really a nitwit in this regard. She is very wrong. I am not sure what made people think that exercising will reduce your energy. On the contrary, what I realized was that I had more energy, and my endurance increased, which also meant that I wanted more time with Desiree. I am sure that a part of her regretted asking me to 'shape up' because it made me want to dance with her all night long. This time, I had the endurance of a mule to do it. She struggled and struggled, but she could not cope. I told you guys that I am a strong man," Ray remarked, being proud of himself while contracting his biceps.

Adam and Kamal chuckled.

Ray continued. "Seriously, there is another factor that made things worse in that department."

"And what would that be?" Kamal inquired with tongue in cheek.

"Have you been to any gym recently?" Ray asked Kamal.

"No," Kamal responded.

"Well, I sometimes go to the one in the hospital adjacent to the doctor's lounge, and it is almost always empty. It has one treadmill, one elliptical machine, one stationary bike, and some free weights. The television only shows local channels featuring news you are not particularly interested in. It does not have ESPN. It really sucks to be there. It is way too boring." Adam replied.

"I guess that is why nobody goes there," Ray surmised.

"Well, it may be contributing but may not be the whole

story. The truth is that health care workers, like doctors and nurses, sometimes preach what they don't practice themselves, especially in terms of exercise. We always claim to be too busy," Adam explained.

"Anyway, if you go to a gym with public membership, you will understand the problem I ran into. Please bear in mind that I was not getting enough...em...em...great time from Desiree. It was like...I mean, she makes me feel like I was an annoying pebble in her sock while she is in a public gathering where she could not be seen removing her shoes, let alone removing her sock. I felt she was just tolerating me for whatever it is worth. It was so sad. Our quiet time was terribly inadequate. When I go to the gym, I get to do different exercises and even play basketball with guys there. I also tend to exercise longer. Now, I go to the gym and see all these young and super attractive ladies who have come to exercise wearing, you know, one of those...you know...two types of sports apparel.

"What sports apparel?" Adam inquired.

"The first one covers nothing, and the second one does not cover anything," Ray responded

"Really?" Adam remarked with surprise. "Are you just joking?"

"I am very serious! Ray exclaimed. I mean, let us face the truth here. The hot chicks are the ones that go to the gym. That is a fact every guy knows. Okay, so I always try to lower my gaze, but there are mirrors everywhere. Trust me, you do not want to be running on a treadmill while positioned behind or by the side of one of these chicks when she is on an elliptical machine. Remember also that the majority of ladies you see in the gym also tend to be single, they are well educated and simply put, incredibly beautiful. The worst part is that they flaunt their treasures! Those ladies that you would think need to exercise are the ones that do not go to the gym. Think about it, who is the typical lady that you see jogging on the street in your neighborhood, and what is she wearing?" Ray lamented.

Kamal and Adam shook their heads. Kamal remarked, "Yeah, I get your point."

Ray continued. "It was like a revolving door of disaster, a true wheel of misfortune that was going round and round, making me dizzy. So, Desiree says no leave me alone. I go to the gym to exercise and end up seeing more desirable and younger chicks who are displaying their treasures. It always felt as if these chicks came to give me a heart attack. I end up coming back home with an astronomically increased desire that will not be fulfilled by Desiree. It was really driving me crazy. The problem is that I know that I need both forms of exercise...for my health, and for my well-being, not just for prevention of diseases, right, Doc?"

"Yeah, I agree." Adam concurred.

"I still go to the gym, but I get discouraged. I never really stopped trying to be close to Desiree," Ray lamented.

"Of course!" Kamal remarked chuckling.

"You are not serious! I am sure you know what I mean," Ray responded.

"Of course! Yes. We know what you mean," Kamal replied.

The three of them started laughing.

"My relationship with Desiree has been mountains and valleys, up and down like a yo-yo. We can be happy soul mates for two days, and suddenly, she will turn against me and make me wonder why I am still married to her for the next week. Among the worst moments happened the weekend before Thanksgiving holiday. After a very good night, and I mean a *very* good night...."

Adam and Kamal chuckled.

"I am serious. It was a very good night," Ray tried to explain.

"Of course, yes! It was a very good night. We can tell," Kamal remarked while laughing.

"Anyway, we had an eventful night, a night of sweet surrender, a night of soft and tender, a night of giving in without giving up, a night of agreeing with and agreeing to. I told Desiree that the night was special for two reasons, and she lovingly asked, "What is reason number one?" I replied, "I am with you." And she asked while smiling, "And what is reason number two?" I replied, "You are with me."

"Awwww!!!!" Adam remarked in jest while crossing his hands over his heart.

"The truth is, we are supposed to be having that kind of night on a regular basis, maybe six or seven nights a week. In the morning, I followed her to the kitchen to help. We were just having fun while cooking together."

"You cooked?" Adam inquired in jest.

"Okay! She cooked, and I pretended to be helping her with the cooking," Ray responded. "Are you happy now, Doctor Prosecutor?"

"I just wanted to get the facts straight so that I don't have to charge you for perjury," Adam countered.

Ray simply ignored him, faced Kamal and continued his talk, "When she brought out the flour, I asked her whether we were making cakes or pancakes. She replied with, 'To cake or to pancake? That is the question,' which I thought was very funny. So, I started to ad-lib a song using a serving spoon as a microphone, and she used the spatula as her microphone, and we started singing together, making up the words as we went along. It was a lot of fun."

Cake or pancake
Let us take it, take it
Let us shake it, shake it
Let us mix it, mix it
Let us turn it, turn it

(Ray)
Show it to me, babe
Shake it for me babe
Bring it to me babe
Give it to me babe

(Desiree)
Hang on tight
Hold me tight
Squeeze me tight
Do me right

The pap, the pop, the pump up, the pup

Let us bake it bake it
Let us make it, make it
Let us flip it, flip it
Let us do it, do it

(Ray)
Show it to me, babe
Shake it for me babe
Bring it to me babe
Give it to me babe

(Desiree)
Hang on tight
Hold me tight
Squeeze me tight
Do me right

The pap, the pop, the pump up, the pup

We are grooving, grooving
We are moving, moving
We are loving, loving
We are proving, proving our love

(Ray)
Show it to me babe
Shake it for me babe
Bring it to me babe
Give it to me babe

(Desiree)
Hang on tight
Hold me tight
Squeeze me tight
Do me right

The pap, the pop, the pump up, the pup

"She was really enjoying herself dancing with me."

"She was enjoying herself?" Kamal interrupted.

"Okay, I was enjoying it too. Are you happy now, Mr. Desiree's Defender? What's up with both of you? Did she bribe both of you? Anyway, I mean, it was great. Honestly, I had forgotten that she could dance. I don't even remember the last time we danced together. My guess will be…at somebody's wedding party probably more than ten years previously. We were really going at the dance uninhibited, and at some point, she turned around, and I held her by the waist. and we both looked up towards the living room only to see that all the children were watching us with their mouths wide open with surprise."

Adam and Kamal started laughing.

"I mean, their jaws were touching the floor in amazement. We had no idea how long they were there. They certainly have never seen us dance before. They did not see it coming. Honestly, we did not see it coming, either. I tell you though, it was a lot of fun. Then Bryan remarked that maybe we should be on the Dancing with the Stars show. Paige then responded that the show typically featured a celebrity who is the star and asked who the star will be in our case. Patricia then responded that it was obvious that the star is daddy because he is the one who is working."

"Oh no!" Kamal remarked.

"I had to correct Patricia immediately that the fact that her mum is a homemaker does not mean she is not working. I tried to highlight what their mother has been doing for them."

"What did Desiree say?" Kamal inquired.

"She said 'really?' after hearing what Patricia said. Subsequently, she remained silent throughout not uttering a word, but I knew that it bothered her a great deal. However, I wasn't too sure what to do. I mean, you would think that a girl would have more appreciation for the sacrifice of a well-educated homemaker mum who is taking care of her family. It is so disappointing in the way people these days do not have any appreciation. I think part of it is due to the hypocritical changes in our modern society, which is pushing for women to abandon their traditional roles and then complain that children are not well brought up. It is hypocrisy everywhere. It is very unfortunate," Ray concluded.

The true star
Your affection took me
To a wonderful state
From the very start

Your warmth enables me
To be in a calm state
Even when we're apart

For your love guided me
To a happy place
Like Polaris, the North Star

You are truly the shining star
The sparkling diamond in my sky
An admiration for those who are far
An absolute delight for those who are near

Desiree, you will always be the star in my life

"I kept wondering how to get through to Desiree. I have always tried to have a good relationship with her and minimize conflict. I also try to surprise her once in a while. It is just that she sometimes does not see things the way I see them. Or perhaps, things do not go exactly as I planned them, or they just don't turn out the way I had envisaged," Ray lamented.

"What did you mean?" Ray asked Kamal.

"Take for example, during the Thanksgiving holiday, a few days after the *Dancing with the Stars* imbroglio, I decided to cook breakfast to give her some kitchen time off. You know that I am the *Chef of the Year* when it comes to breakfast," Ray opined.

"Oh yeah! That will be according to *The Starvation Magazine,*" Kamal stated in jest. "So, what did you prepare for them?"

"I think it was cereal, boiled eggs, and I toasted the bread," Ray explained with a sense of pride.

"That is what earned you the *Chef of the Year* award?" Adam asked.

"Interesting! You really think of yourself as a lean, mean, cooking machine," Kamal remarked while laughing.

"I know they all enjoyed my treat whether you guys believe in my cooking skills or not," Ray concluded.

"So, were they hard-boiled eggs or soft-boiled eggs?" Kamal inquired.

"What is the difference?" Ray inquired, looking stunned.

Adam and Kamal looked at each other. "You are the *Chef of the Century* indeed!" Kamal remarked.

"Seriously, is there a difference or are you guys just pulling my leg?" Ray asked.

"There is a difference," Kamal replied.

"Really? I don't know. I just leave the eggs in boiling water until I see that at least one of the eggs has cracked. Then I know that they are all done, and all the Salmonella bacteria are dead," Ray explained.

Adam and Kamal started laughing. Ray initially kept quiet, but later joined the laughter being unable to control himself.

"Anyway, since, we were not expecting any guests, I decided to surprise Desiree and offered to take care of the Thanksgiving meal. She protested that it would be a lot for me to do so we negotiated back and forth on what I should do. Eventually, she gave in after much persuasion from me that I wanted it to be special. So, we agreed that I would take care of the turkey. The turkey was already thawing in the fridge. So later in the morning, Desiree and the kids went back to sleep after breakfast. I was thinking of something to surprise her. While I was on the sofa watching the early morning shows, I fell asleep too. By the time I woke up, the first football game was already in the second quarter with *Detroit Lions* trailing by ten points. I was watching the game when I suddenly remembered my promise to Desiree that I would take care of the turkey. So, I took out the turkey which was fully thawed at this time.

However, instead of cooking it, I had a great idea to dress the turkey in a surprising show of love for Desiree."

"Please don't tell me that you actually put some clothes on the turkey as your way of dressing it," Kamal remarked in jest.

"And used some of the lipsticks and mascara that Desiree did not use on the turkey," Adam chimed in.

"Of course not! I am not stupid," Ray replied.

Adam and Kamal looked at each other and raised their eyebrows.

"What he meant was that he is not that stupid," Adam clarified facing Kamal who nodded in agreement without uttering a word.

"I decided to have a loving fun with Desiree using the turkey. Then, I went to wake Desiree up. When she looked at the clock and realized that it was well into the afternoon, she jumped to her feet and asked me about the turkey immediately. It was as if she was dreaming of the turkey. Instead of answering her question, I enthusiastically told her that I have a big surprise for her."

"Okay. Did the turkey wake up and...run away?" Desiree asked me while trying to smell the air for the aroma of cooked turkey.

"Very funny," I replied. "I guess that is why they cut the head, the neck, and the feet of the turkey but they still tie the legs together—to make sure the turkey doesn't run away while it is in the freezer."

"I am sure her heart was beating fast," Adam opined. "Maybe she was having a nightmare or since she was sleeping during the day, maybe we can call it *Desiree's Daymare: The escape of the Thanksgiving turkey.* You guys should make it into a movie."

Ray simply ignored him and continued, "I told her to relax, and then she asked me if there were firefighters in the kitchen. I told her to close her eyes and used a blindfold to heighten the surprise. After a weakly spirited protest, she eventually agreed. I led her to the kitchen, and I uncovered her eyes to show her the surprise I made with the turkey. To my utmost surprise, instead of appreciating my gesture, she looked initially quite shocked. In a matter of nanoseconds, her mood changed. She looked at the clock, then she looked at me, then looked at the clock and looked at me then she looked at the turkey. When her eyes returned to me for the third time, her eyes were red with indescribable anger. She stared at me as if I was crazy or something. Then she had...this unbelievable emotional wintry mix of...anger, sadness, and disappointment that was difficult to characterize. She shouted at me, 'What did you do?' I mean, the way she raised her hands and her voice, you would have thought that she would surely strangle me."

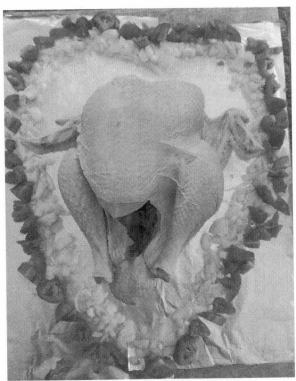

Thanksgiving is love. Nothing beats love at Thanksgiving...except lack of appreciation from your lover.

"I was confused initially. I thought it was obvious that I had made a love symbol around the turkey using cut pieces of tomato and onions to express my love for her."

"Obviously, she did not appreciate it," Adam expressed.

"Not at all. She accused me of being unreasonable. So much for romance! So much for being spontaneous! It is ridiculous," Ray lamented.

"So, what happened to the turkey?" Kamal asked.

"After her lack of appreciation, I left the kitchen to avoid conflict. I went to watch the rest of the football games on television. She eventually cut up the turkey, boiled the pieces and fried them lightly. It was delicious, but I was not so pleased with what happened."

Ray took a sip of his drink and continued his ranting. "Women will say that they love guys who are romantic and spontaneous, and when you are romantic and spontaneous, all they do is to make you regret it. Some women are just mood killers. Desiree is the number one mood killer known to mankind."

"It was unfortunate," Kamal opined.

"I mean a woman will note that her husband is trying to woo her, but she will just kill the mood and then wonder why her husband is not spontaneous and romantic. Imagine, I once read about a lady who saw her husband put a breath mint in his mouth, and she sensed that he is going to want a kiss, so she dashed to the kitchen and ate some garlic to discourage the husband from advancing to her. When the marriage counselor asked her why she did that, she responded that it was not the kiss she was afraid of, but what he may want to do afterward. I was screaming, "H-E-L-L-O!!!" at my I-pad when I was reading the article. I thought she should be happy that her husband wanted to be with her."

"It is really sad," Adam expressed.

"Well, I do not believe that there has ever been any woman who ever lived on this planet who knows how to kill a romantic mood like Desiree," Ray opined.

"What do you mean?" Adam inquired.

"I tell you, if there were a mood-killing competition as an

event in the Olympics, Desiree would win in every category whether it is with the eyes, with words, with action...I mean...she will win any category," Ray suggested.

"Wow! Is it that bad?" Kamal expressed surprise.

"Yeah. It is probably even worse."

"If I didn't know you quite a bit, I may think that you are exaggerating," Kamal responded.

"There is no exaggeration here, bro! It is pain, nothing but excruciating pain. Take, for example, Desiree's mum called on a Friday and asked us to bring the children the following day for them to have some family time with their cousins. Desiree's brother had come to town with his wife and children, and Nana decided to have a party for the children. To me, it was a break from those children because I will get to have my wife to myself for a change. So, that fine Saturday morning after Desiree left to drop the children off, I spontaneously thought of a romantic idea that I was sure would knock her clothes off. I put the temperature of the house at 80 degrees Fahrenheit and increased the temperature of our bedroom to 90 degrees Fahrenheit."

Adam and Kamal were puzzled and looked at each other without uttering a word.

Ray continued his tale of woes. "When I heard that Desiree was opening the door, I quickly dashed to the bedroom to put on my show. She entered and immediately remarked that the house was hot. I heard her in the bedroom, but I did not respond."

"Ray! Ray! Where are you?" Desiree inquired.

"Here, babe," Ray responded from the bedroom trying his impersonation of Barry White's deep voice.

"It is very hot in here!" Desiree remarked as she quickened her steps into the bedroom.

"Yes, babe. I am hot, and so are you." Ray responded with a smile.

Desiree ignored his comments and went straight to the windows to open them. She then reduced the thermostat to 70 degrees Fahrenheit.

"Why are you staying in this hot bedroom?" Desiree asked with genuine concern.

Ray then laid out his perfect romantic line which he had been working on. "I got very hot waiting for your love, my dear. Now, you are here to cool me down."

My ongoing ordeal

My baby
Can you feel the heat of my love?
My darling
Can you feel the beat of my love?
My honey
Can you feel my heart pumping?
My sugar,
Can you feel my heart beating?

Something great overwhelms me
Every time that you are near me
I love the feeling of it
And I want more of it

"Wow!" Adam remarked. "So, what did she say?"

"Nothing!" Ray responded.

"What did you mean by nothing?" Adam inquired again.

"She simply shook her head in disbelief, took her purse and her car keys and headed for the door to go back to her kids."

Adam and Kamal chuckled in unison.

"What?" Ray asked in a loud voice.

"Nothing!" Kamal responded.

"Did I do something wrong?" Ray inquired with sincerity.

"Absolutely not!" Kamal responded and started laughing. Adam also joined in the laughter.

"You guys are crazy," Ray remarked.

"No. You are the one who is crazy, crazy, and crazy," Kamal responded.

"What did you mean? I was only trying to be romantic and spontaneous."

"Yeah, you were, but in a weird guy way," Kamal answered him.

"Rubbish!" Ray replied and retorted, "So, what is the non-weird guy way of doing it?"

"I don't know," Kamal responded. "It just felt...somehow off."

"Did you think that I should have left the bedroom very cold instead, so that when she walks in and complain that it was too cold, then I would respond that I was there to keep her warm?"

"Hmmm!" Adam sighed.

"What?" Ray asked again.

"I think she would still leave," Kamal opined.

"How can a guy then be romantic, spontaneous, and unexpected at the same time?" Ray expressed.

"I don't know," Kamal responded. "Maybe it depends on the lady."

"Maybe ask the lady what will turn her on—" Adam suggested as he was interrupted by Ray who disagreed vehemently.

"C' mon! What is the use of asking her? Asking her will ruin the spontaneous and unexpected part of the romance," Ray explained.

"But being spontaneous in your style has not worked either," Adam reminded him.

"Why would you ask a lady what will surprise her? I think it will be a disaster," Ray reiterated.

"What do you mean?" Kamal sought clarification.

"I am sure most ladies will probably change the tone of their voice to the one that they already know makes you lose your head and your mind." Ray cleared his throat and started imitating a lady talking in a seductive voice *'Honey! You are so nice! Darling, a simple Emerald-Cut Emerald and Diamond Pear-Shaped Halo ring in 18 karat white gold will really surprise me, and a nice three tier diamond bracelet will surely make me perspire the hot sweat of immeasurable love. However, if you make it a trifecta with an addition of a diamond necklace, it will truly be an amazing trifecta perfecta that will take my breath away forever.'* She will probably stretch her beautiful fingers of her left hand to you while touching you seductively with her right hand to make you stop thinking completely."

Adam and Kamal started laughing uncontrollably.

Ray continued. "There are many things about diamonds

that lasts forever. It is just different for different people."

"Why will it be different for people?" Adam sought clarification.

Ray shook his head and chuckled. "For the village where the multinational companies go to mine the diamonds, the community conflict lasts forever. For the mining company, the profit lasts forever. For the lady who was given the diamond, the sparkle lasts forever. For the guy who bought the diamond, he hopes that her love lasts forever, but rather, it is the debt that lasts forever!"

"Poor guy!" Adam lamented.

> **Author's note:** To our ladies: Do you like your man to be romantic? Spontaneous? Unexpected? What will that look like, and how should he go about it? If you don't, what would you suggest to him to rock your world?

Ray continued his narration. "Anyway, I caught up to her at the main door of the house and requested that at least, we can go to lunch together being careful not to call it a lunch-date, as this may scare her away. I don't know. I never could understand her. She had not prepared any lunch, and so, it was not so difficult to convince her."

Ray quickly dressed up with the hope that something milder like casual lunch may eventually lead to something greater when they get back.

"So, where would you want us to go for lunch?" Ray inquired from Desiree.

"It does not matter to me," Desiree replied.

"Great. We will go to Tasty Bites on Western Avenue," Ray concluded.

"No. I don't want to go to Tasty Bites," Desiree responded.

"I thought you said that it doesn't matter where we went just now," Ray reminded her.

Desiree did not respond. She just looked out of the window on the passenger side of the car and shrugged her shoulders.

"What about Fast Bites on the First street?"

Desiree shook her head in negativity.

"Well, we can go to Fresh Bakes on Seventh Street," Ray suggested.

"I don't like Fresh Bakes. Their baked products are not fresh enough," Desiree opined again.

Ray sighed, trying to bottle up his annoyance.

"So, where exactly do you really want to go?" Ray asked her again.

"Anywhere else is fine with me," Desiree responded.

"Anywhere else is not fine with you," Ray disagreed, raising his voice in the process.

"You don't need to shout at me," Desiree countered.

Ray sunk his head on the steering wheel of the car, inadvertently blowing the car's horn in the process with huge disappointment written in bold letters on his face. Yet, he was still determined to make it work rather than calling the lunch off and going back into the house.

"Okay. Where would you prefer out of Three Guys Burger, Fish and Chips, Chicken et al, or Sandwich R Us," Ray asked Desiree after he had calmed down.

"Sandwich R Us," Desiree replied.

Ray drove off to the nearest Sandwich R Us on Woodlawn Avenue. They sat down and were given the food menu by the waiter. Ray asked Desiree to order for both of them, but she declined and asked Ray to order instead.

Ray then asked the waiter to get them two Executive Chicken Sandwiches with Tornado dressing, coleslaw, and spicy fries. As the waiter started writing the orders down, Desiree remarked that she did not want a chicken sandwich.

Ray could not hold back anymore. He looked at Desiree and started ranting.

"So, what exactly do you want? Huh! What do you want? Tasty Bites? No Tasty Bites. Fast Bites? No Fast Bites. Maybe you prefer to go for *Frost Bites* instead. Did you really come back home itching for a fight instead? Or is it that you are already missing your kids after only one hour that made you think that misbehaving with me is appropriate?"

Ray's loud comments attracted the attention of other

diners, and they wondered what was going on at their table. The waiter quickly stepped in and reassured Ray that it was okay for her to order something else.

"I will have just the fish sandwich," Desiree finally responded.

"Throughout lunch, we did not say a word to each other. We finished eating and we drove home. As soon as I parked the car, she got into her car and drove away to Nana's place. I felt black and blue, used and abused," Ray concluded.

"That did not go well at all," Adam observed.

"Not at all. The episode that still leaves a bitter taste in my mouth occurred a few weekends afterward. We were together at home. She left herself as disheveled as you can imagine all day. Then in the afternoon, around 5 pm, she decided to take a shower while I was in the living room. I came into the bedroom as she was exiting the master's bathroom with only her towel under her armpits. Her hair was silky wet and was shining, her skin looked so smooth, and the fragrance from her shower soap gave the fresh aura of recently cut grass. It is hard to believe that four kids have come out already through her into this world. She looked so beautiful and inviting. She looked...so amazingly hot with a capital H."

Adam and Kamal looked at each other and smiled.

"So, I was looking at her and smiling...you know... waiting for her to release her towel, hoping she will let it fall to the ground when she starts applying her body cream so I can go from seeing the good part, to seeing the better part, in anticipation of us getting to the best part. She suddenly noticed that I was looking at her, you know...."

Kamal and Adam chuckled.

"You would not believe what happened next," Ray expressed.

"What happened?" Kamal inquired.

"She took her cream and ran into the walk-in clothes closet to cream her body, locking the door behind her. What's up with that?"

Adam and Kamal laughed.

"Man! She ran very fast into that closet. I am pretty sure

Hussein Bolt probably never moved that fast in any race. I tried to get into the closet with her, but she did not open the door until she finished dressing up. Of course, I accused her of being a romantic mood killer," Ray concluded.

Adam and Kamal looked at each other and then looked at Ray, trying to sympathize with his predicament.

Ray continued, "Then she fought back, accusing me of choosing the wrong moment. She argued that we had been home all day and I was busy watching one stupid football game after another and just when she was about to leave the house. Then I suddenly realized that she is at home and I wanted, you know, something...something...from her. I explained that it is not like that, but she insisted, querying why I didn't leave the football game when it was still going on. She stated that it was only after the game was over that I chose to come and disrupt her plans."

"Well, it is because she did not understand how the mind of a guy works," Kamal reasoned.

"Let's face it. It is hard to really blame her." Adam chimed in.

"Why not?" Ray snarled.

"Tell me. How would she know that if she had come to you after taking a shower in a towel during any of the football games, you probably would have just recorded the football game and go for a live-action with her instead? After all, catching the playback of the game later is not a difficult task. You could even watch only the highlights and be okay. She wouldn't understand, would she?" Adam asked Ray.

"I think the bigger problem is that women quite often fail to realize how vividly visual guys are. If a man is looking at his wife, she should kill him with love. I mean, there is a reason why men spend a lot of money to go to adult entertainment of looking, not touching, right? So, if a man is then looking at his wife with the same intensity, why not let him enjoy it. After all, it is not that they prefer him to go look at somebody else anyway," Kamal opined.

"The accusation that I waited all day until she was leaving the house was very absurd. There is no denying the fact that she looked very different when she was just at home versus when she was about to leave the house. I mean, is she trying to impress somebody else outside the house when I am right here at home with her? If anything, she should be trying to impress me. She supposed to be flaunting her treasures for me. I am the one who is entitled to everything desirable…from the luscious hair on her scalp to the baby soft soles of her feet and all the exquisite goodies in the middle."

Ray took a sip of his drink and continued, "Let's face it. If a hungry man is an angry man, then a thirsty man is a pissed off man. However, an intimacy deprived man is an incredibly angry, seriously pissed off, and totally deranged monster who nobody, including himself, knows what erratic decision he is going to make. A wise wife knows that this is not a good gamble because there is absolutely no decision that he will make that will not be inimical to her interest."

"I agree 100%," Adam concurred.

"Hmmm!" Ray sighed. "It was especially painful that day," Ray recalled.

"Why? What made it special?" Adam inquired.

"Early that morning, I was the guest of honor at the *Rising Stars' Breakfast* meeting. This is a monthly community program where the youth assembly invites older achieving men and women to have an informal breakfast with them. It is a mentoring program where successful people are invited to share their experiences and encourage others. I guess I was invited because of my stellar qualifications; being a lawyer, a family man with children, and one who has been married for "eternity."

Ray made air quotes when he mentioned "eternity."

He continued, "To these young people, being married for over ten years is an eternity. I guess they thought that I must be doing something right. In fact, the moderator introduced me as a man of vision with a mission that has been put into action for the greater good of mankind."

"Are you sure he was talking about you?" Kamal asked with tongue in cheek.

"Of course, I am all that and then some more," Ray remarked while laughing. "I am a gift to mankind."

"Tell that to Desiree!" Kamal expressed with a snarl.

"Little do they know what you are just putting up with, in reality," Adam remarked.

"Well, I wouldn't tell them that," Ray responded with a perky smile. "If I did, it will be disastrous for them. They may never grow up, and if they did, they might be too scared to get married. It was even more important to give them positive vibes especially considering the topic I was given."

"What did you speak about?" Kamal inquired.

"I was asked to give a 30-minute talk entitled *Moving up the food chain,*" Ray responded.

"That was quite imaginative," Kamal remarked.

"Yeah! It was quite interesting. I kept it real for them. I made it clear that it is difficult to move up in life. However, a lot of times, it is not gravity that is holding you down. I told the young men that they need to do two FTEs, one after the other. I explained that the first FTE stands for 'Full Time Employment.' They need to study hard, get a good education, work hard, and get wonderful high paying jobs so that they can be gainfully employed. The second FTE was for them to 'Fertilize The Eggs' which means that they should get married and have busloads of children. This made them laugh hysterically. I told them not to think that marriage will slow them down. Then, I asked them by a show of hands, how many were married. To my surprise, less than 20% of eligible bachelors were married. So, I tried to chat them up a bit, and I asked those who were not married what the problems were."

"Of course, they were either waiting for the right partner or waiting for the right time," Adam chimed in.

"That is what you think. I asked them, saying, 'are you playing hard-to-get, or are you having selection crises?' This made them laugh. One of the guys jokingly asked me what I meant. So, I decided to expand the conversation and told them that, 'Playing hard to get is when you have potential candidates, and you pretend not to be interested so that you will not be thought of as being easy and you do this for so long that many good candidates just leave you singing Bob Marley on their way out.'"

"What did you mean by singing Bob Marley?" Adam inquired.

"I don't wanna wait in vain for your love," Ray replied. "It was a classic song. Anyway, I informed them that on the other hand, having a selection crisis is not being satisfied with the candidates at your disposal. You keep wishing you could graft that feature onto that person, remove that quality from that candidate and thereby, assemble your dream spouse who is exactly that—a dream spouse, not a real one."

"Well, playing hard-to-get will apply more to ladies and selection crises is always a problem for shallow guys," Adam opined.

"You can be deep and still have selection crises. It is a matter of contentment," Kamal voiced his opinion.

"Then I turned to the guys and told them that I have news for those who were having selection crises in trying to marry the most beautiful woman in the world. I told them to simply admit that they lost because...she is married. They reacted with a surprised look on their faces and then I told them that I married her. This made them all chuckled."

Adam and Kamal chuckled too. They did not say a word but gestured as if they did not want to get into a controversy.

Ray raised his voice as if to be emphatic that what he said was true. "Yes. Of course, I married the most beautiful lady in the world because I told her that she is the most beautiful lady in the world. Did you think I was lying?"

At this, Adam could no longer control himself, and he responded. "No, you are not lying to me. You were lying to yourself, which means it is okay so long it stays in your head."

"It is a fact, and I am entitled to it. Desiree is the most beautiful lady in the world," Ray insisted.

"It is a farce and you are entitled to it because Nora is the most beautiful lady in the world," Adam asserted.

Kamal thought of telling his buddies that they were just drunk on optimism juice. After all, he knows that Bonita is the most beautiful lady in the world. Furthermore, she is the only one whose name also means "beautiful." It was very clear to him that she wears the crown. He wanted to speak but decided to be more mature about it and simply remarked, "You guys are still teenagers. You are like two stupid love drunk guys who are fighting over a pretty chick, but the chick is actually dating another guy."

Ray and Adam looked at Kamal with a fake angry look. Ray made a fist, while Adam clenched his teeth as if they were poised to fight Kamal together.

Kamal ignored their dirty look and remarked while turning to Ray, "You want to fight for Desiree who you claim will be the world champion in *No, leave me alone* category among married women. He then turned to Adam and remarked: "and you Adam, you want to break your neck for Nova who will win the Olympic gold medal in the *No, leave me alone* category among single ladies."

Ray shook his head in partial defeat and remarked, "Well, I know what I know."

Adam stretched out his hands towards Ray as if consoling him. "I sympathize with Ray. He does not know what he doesn't know because he only knows what he knows."

Kamal shook his head and remarked, "It is okay. I am not mad at both of you and in actual fact, I forgive you. I really have heartfelt sympathy for both of you. I mean, both of you needed the denial to keep going, because I am sure that you know that Bonita is actually the most beautiful lady in the world."

The three of them started laughing.

> **Author's note:** Sorry ladies. Every husband always tries to convince himself that he married the most beautiful woman in the world. It is a guy thing! However, as you can see from this section that none of these guys married the most beautiful woman in the world. **The author of this novel did**. Well, what do you expect? I am a guy too (smile).

Ray concluded his story from the breakfast meeting that he encouraged the participants to do their best and bring their A-game into everything they do at all times. "It was a very interesting interaction with the leaders of tomorrow. So, you can imagine how devastating it was for me when the same

Desiree treated me like she did on this very day!"

Ray took a sip of his drink and continued. "The following Saturday was an Organization for Oppressed Husbands (OOH!) meeting in Annapolis. It was very interesting, to say the least. We had two new members who were still married but wanted some suggestions from the experienced folks like us."

Kamal chuckled.

Ray ignored him and continued. "The first guy's name is Peyton. He told us that he wanted to learn how not to *compromise*. We were surprised, and somebody quickly corrected him that to *compromise* with one's spouse is a very good thing, and it is essential for a happy marriage. Then, he told us that he wanted to achieve the same, but he feels that he is being taken for a ride in the name of *compromise*."

"I am not following," remarked Adam.

"Well, same for us too until he explained what he meant. He said that it appeared that the word *compromise* is only used by his wife when he agrees with her and they ended up doing what she wanted. For instance, when their first child was to go to kindergarten, there were two schools close to their apartment complex. His wife preferred the *Prestige Kindergarten* which according to her is where the who's who in the neighborhood apartment complex send their children, but he preferred the *Mighty Acorn Kindergarten* because they have more rigorous academia, and it was even cheaper by a few hundred bucks a month. In the end, they reached a *compromise,* and they sent him to *Prestige Kindergarten*. When they wanted to buy a house, he wanted them to buy a very nice townhouse in a very good neighborhood, but she wanted them to buy a single-family house with plenty of grass. They went back and forth on it. In the end, they reached a *compromise,* and they bought the single-family house. Then there was the time that their children wanted to have a pet. He suggested that they get a dog, but his wife wanted them to get a cat. He explained to her that a dog can guard the house and can play with the children. Moreover, he is allergic to cats. She insisted that she didn't want a dog because somebody must walk it and be cleaning after it outside. "What will happen if you were not at home?" She asked rhetorically. In the end, they reached a *compromise,* and they got two cats. He told us that they now have six cats at home because his wife had 'accidentally' bought a male and a female cat. Now, he has been taking allergy pills every day because of the cats. The breaking point for Peyton came about two months previously when he wanted to change his car from an old beat-up Toyota Corolla. He had been saving up some money and finally, he was going to trade in his car for a three-year old, four-door Toyota Camry sedan with leather seats. To his surprise, his wife insisted that he buys another minivan instead so that if there is a problem with the minivan she drives, they can drive his car. He said that he drew the red line right there. His wife became cold at home. She kept saying to him that he did not care about her. She accused him of having a heart of stone, and that he did not care about her emotions or about his children."

"How many children do they have?" Kamal inquired.

"Three," Ray responded.

"But they can all fit in a Camry. It can seat five people comfortably. Peyton and his wife in the front and the three kids can sit in the back," Adam opined.

"That was our opinion too, and Peyton said that he made that point to his wife, but she kept saying that the trunk of the Camry is not big enough for them, especially if they wanted to go grocery shopping," Ray continued.

"What!" Adam exclaimed. "Was she planning to buy the supermarket in one trip? Moreover, it is his car. Were they not coping with the Corolla?"

Ray shrugged his shoulders and continued. "Well, in the end, they reached a *compromise,* and he bought a Dodge Caravan minivan instead. Peyton then went to the window, moved the curtains, and pointed at a blue minivan across the street for us to see. He said that every time he gets inside the minivan, he feels like a loser."

"Poor guy!" Adam remarked.

"So, what did you 'elders' suggest?" Kamal inquired while making air quotes on mentioning elders.

"We were stunned, but before we could react, the other

new guy, Tom, stated that he has similar problems, So, we listened to him too. Tom stated that in his case, before he got married, he read a self-help book on marital affairs that broke down how marriage should work. The author suggested that men should never let it be in doubt as per who is in charge. The author emphasized that the husband should make the decision on major issues, and the buck stops with him. So, he took this philosophy into his marriage, and he and his wife agreed to it that he would decide on major issues, and the wife will decide minor issues."

"An interesting division of labor, I must say," expressed Kamal.

"Well, that is what you'll think. Tom mentioned that they have been married for eighteen years, and he has not been in the position to make any decision whatsoever. His wife dubbed every decision as minor. Whether it was which school the children should go, what they should do for summer programs, what house they would buy, where they would go for vacations, et cetera. You name it, she would quickly classify it as minor and make the decision. The most recent issue occurred when their eldest daughter was to start college. He preferred her to go to his alma mater, University of Lanham, but his wife wanted her to go to the University of Greenbelt. She is now a freshman at the University of Greenbelt. She did not even apply to the University of Lanham at all."

Adam and Kamal chuckled. "What will then qualify as a major decision for his wife?" Kamal asked with tongue in cheek.

"We were curious too, and we asked him. He said that when he disagreed with her on the same point, she told him that if they wanted to buy an airplane and they needed to decide between a Boeing 747 or Airbus A380, she would absolutely know that it is really a major decision and her husband should decide that," Ray reported.

The three guys started laughing hysterically. "So, what did the elders recommend?" Kamal inquired while making air quotes again.

"For Peyton, we advised him to stick to his gun if he is

deciding about something for himself. For Tom, we suggested to him to negotiate a change to the rules. From now on, he will be making the minor decisions, and she can make the major decisions," Ray reported.

Kamal and Adam looked at each other with a puzzled affect, and Kamal asked, "What if she changed what is now major and what is now minor after the negotiation process?"

"Hmm! We did not consider that," Ray regretted.

"Poor guy!" Adam commented.

"Don't feel sorry for them. They are fine. Tom is in cruise control, at least until the next decision—but Peyton snapped," Ray continued.

"What happened?" Kamal asked, surprised.

"About a month later at another OOH meeting, Peyton looked full of life. He told us that one day on his way home from work, he passed by a Ford car dealership. Out of the blue, he decided to go and see the sales representative."

Kamal chuckled, knowing that a bombshell was coming.

Ray continued. "He said that he traded-in the minivan on-the-spot for a brand new, factory fresh, flaming hot cherry red Ford Mustang GT Premium convertible with all the bells and whistles. He said that he felt his *mojo* was restored after he bought the car. He walked to the window triumphantly and moved the curtains for us to see the red Mustang parked on the road tempting every guy to take it for a spin. We were happy for him. That is how you get your balls back!"

"I can't wait to hear what happened when he got home that day," Adam stated in an impatient expectation.

"He told us that when his wife saw the Mustang, she screamed. Peyton said that he did not care. She could get a megaphone if she liked. She accused him of being impulsive. He just ignored her. She accused him of being self-centered and asked what will happen if her minivan has any problem. That question got his attention, and it made him reply to her, breaking his code of silence."

"What did he say?" Adam inquired.

"He said that he told her that he doesn't care what she does. She could call a tow truck, taxi, Uber, Lyft, Carry, or Move. It is her problem. If she likes, she could call ghostbusters too."

"What a shame! She pushed her husband to a breaking point with her uncompromising *I must always win* attitude," Kamal remarked.

"She has the classic *my way* or the *highway* attitude. Now, her husband has taken the *highway* in a Mustang convertible, and he is enjoying the speed and the breeze. He is never going to give that up for her," Adam predicted.

"Yeah. You are right. Now she is appealing to him to get the Toyota Camry, but he refused. He told her that if they have some money, they could buy a relatively inexpensive 4-door sedan as a spare car in the future, but his car is the Mustang. End of story. In any case, he bought a 6-speed manual transmission Mustang GT knowing fully well that his wife can only drive an automatic transmission vehicle. So, he is not worried about his wife taking his *baby* for a ride. He told us that his wife is not happy with him, but that doesn't bother him at all. Now, he is happy with himself."

"Honestly, I think guys should take the opinions of their wives into consideration while they make decisions that they feel have a substantial impact on themselves and their families. However, men do not have to bend over backward every time while trying to please their wives. Some women just never stop making outrageous demands. They push and push until the guy throws his hands in the air and fights back. Sometimes these guys with bruised egos and badly damaged self-confidence then make extreme decisions to compensate for losses they felt they suffered. Such is what happened with Peyton here. He is a simple guy who wanted to pay for a used Camry with four doors that could serve the family and possibly avoid having a car note. Now, he over-reacted and bought a two-door sports car that only he can drive. He is definitely going to be paying car notes and higher insurance costs. Yet, he is not going to care anymore. Men! I agree with the 'elders,' guys need to make decisions for themselves. Everything must not be about pleasing the wife. Sometimes, a guy just has to apply the principle: *let the lady have her say* and *let the guy have his way*," Adam opined.

"Let's face it. Most decisions are going to be made by the wife anyway, whether we like it or not. So, for a happy marriage, ladies need to understand that for that *one thing* that he is particularly interested in, *let him have it*. In the end, most husbands will be happy with almost anything, so long as they are not being bothered. It doesn't take a lot to please a man. On the other hand, women are just too crafty. There is nothing simple about them. Women can be impossible to understand, and they change their minds very frequently. The worst part is that they don't see anything wrong with them changing their minds. If a woman wants to be mischievous, she will outwit virtually every man she targets. If a woman tells you that something is simple, it is not true, and if she tells you that it is complicated, it is false. The sad part is that she may not be trying to lie to you. It is just that the way they process information and act is totally different from our way," Kamal lamented.

He then looked at Adam and remarked that every man should say to himself, "I need a…I need a…I need a…I need a wife who loves and cares about me. By the way, maturity is an advantage in any relationship."

Adam knew that Kamal's theatrics of "I need a…" is a jab at him trying to reference Aneida as the lady he should marry instead of Nora. He just decided to ignore Kamal and did not comment on what he said. After all, he is entitled to his disordered thinking.

> **Author's note:** Every wife greatly influences her husband and knows how to get whatever she wants from him. However, it takes a smart wife not to make her husband feel that he is being dominated, even when he is.

"What can we do? Tell me. Women are quite challenging to negotiate with because they play on our love and emotional attachment to them. Unfortunately, some of them even want to lord over us because of the daisies in their control," Ray responded.

"Just be nice to her and keep appealing to her. Hopefully, you can bring the best out of her. The challenge is that a lot of time, they are right in their counsel, but a lot of time too, they are just being mischievous, and most of the time, we cannot tell the difference. Unfortunately, as guys, we are just too slow to keep up with them when their cunning act is on full display. The problem is that a wife will always know how to play her husband too well. He does not stand a chance at all."

Kamal took a sip of his drink and continued, "That is why it is important to choose wisely. I advise young men not to just fix their gaze on the front view and the back yard of the ladies, but they should put a lot of emphasis on the brain and the heart too. I know that it is hard for them especially when they are smitten by a twenty-year-old bombshell who is just reaching her full bloom."

Adam knew that Kamal was taking a jab at him again, but he decided not to respond to him.

"You mean they should consider her from top to bottom and from the front to the rear?" Ray inquired jokingly.

"You are not serious!" Kamal replied.

"I am dead serious," Ray responded. "The brain is on top, and the bottom is self-explanatory, ...and by the way, the heart is in the front too...wait, maybe the heart is in the center...."

"When will you ever be serious?" Kamal asked Ray, interrupting him.

Adam interjected before Ray could respond, "He is usually very serious when Desiree is saying her patented *No, leave me alone* to him."

"Yeah right!" Kamal remarked. "You really think that this guy can put his foot down on anything with Desiree?"

"Excuse me. I have put my foot down before, and I will continue to do so as needed," Ray responded with masculine pride.

"Really?" Kamal asked in jest.

"Of course, yes. For example, she preferred us to eat wheat bread and whole-grain bread. I sometimes get tired of them because they taste like cardboard to me sometimes. So, I suggested that maybe an occasional potato bread or white bread will be fine too. However, she would always say *no,* and she wouldn't listen. So, one Saturday morning, I got tired of putting up with this foolishness. I stopped by the supermarket close to our home and I bought two loaves of potato bread. Desiree was livid. I was counter mad at her too, especially that it came after I had endured her incessant *No, leave me alone* and *it is my body* maltreatment all through the night. I told her too that it is *my money, my mouth,* and *my body* and I can do whatever I want with myself. Anyway, what difference does it make if I have a heart attack? After all, a heart attack from what I enjoy cannot be as bad as the heartache from the maltreatment she is giving me. I accused her of being mean to me. I told her that I truly feel used and abused in our marriage. I did not mince words at all," Ray related.

"Did the strategy work?" Adam inquired.

"For me, it did. Because I ate what I wanted. The problem was that the children ate my potato bread in the refrigerator instead of their mother's cardboard wheat bread too. I was mad at them for eating my potato bread. Desiree was mad at them too for eating 'unhealthy bread.' It was unfortunate for our children as it appeared that the only agreement between Desiree and me was being mad at them."

"Poor kids!" remarked Adam.

Ray continued, "I really hate to put our children in this bad situation. It was their mother's fault. If only she was a little more understanding and accommodating...."

"And you were more accommodating too," Kamal interjected.

"I am very accommodating. I have been very accommodating. I have been extremely patient. I have been used and abused by her all these years. In fact, any more accommodating on my part will simply turn me into an accommodation, maybe a hotel or something. I have—"

"You could have simply left your children alone," Kamal interjected again. "They saw you as their champion in the wheat bread versus potato bread fight. That is probably why they took your side and ate the potato bread," Kamal surmised.

"Huh! What an interesting observation!" Ray remarked with an element of surprise in his voice. "I did not see it that way. Hmm. You have given me a totally different perspective."

"That is what friends are for, right?" Kamal expressed.

"Well, I guess you are right. In any case, the house got colder and colder. I did not talk to Desiree for almost a week. I was so fed up with our marriage. One day, I was watching the TV and was busy flipping through channels without watching anything in particular. I watched the conclusion of a *Law and Order* episode and felt that it was what I needed in my marriage with Desiree because she doesn't follow natural marriage *law* and her incessant *No, leave me alone* is totally out of *order*. While I was fuming in anger, The Dr. Phil show came on the air. I remarked to Desiree, who was walking past the sofa, that maybe we should go on Dr. Phil's show. At least an expert can then tell her that she is wrong in the way she has been mistreating me. She simply ignored me. However, about thirty minutes later, she came back to me where I was watching a sporting event that I was not particularly interested in, and she replied that she was open to the idea."

"To go public on Dr. Phil?" Adam asked in utter disbelief.

"I was shocked too because that is what I thought she meant, but she clarified that she meant marital counseling. I suggested that we go back to Mama Wise because, at that point, she was the only sensible marital counselor I knew," Ray explained.

"Did she agree?" Adam inquired.

"Nope! I guess she didn't want to hear the truth."

"Not necessarily," Kamal interjected. "Maybe she just wanted a second opinion."

"Did you mean a forty-second opinion?" Ray asked with a tone of seriousness in his voice.

"Well, maybe she just wanted fresh ideas," Kamal reaffirmed.

"Fresh my foot! There is nothing stale about the fact that wives should take good care of their husbands. You don't need to press a refresh button to know that," Ray emphasized.

"What about the converse, that men should take good care of their wives too?" Kamal asked.

"Well, I agree with you, but I have been taking good care

of her and her kids!" Ray exclaimed.

"Calm down, bro! That is just what you think. Her opinion may be different," Kamal suggested.

"If that is the case, then she must not have any appreciation for all that I have been doing for her and her kids," Ray surmised.

"It doesn't follow. Maybe something is just bothering her, and she does not know how or when to bring it up," Kamal reasoned.

"But mistreating me is not the answer," Ray reiterated.

"I agree," Kamal replied.

"So, you finally understand my point," Ray commented.

"I have always understood you, even if you've been too blind to see it. I just wanted you to try and see things from your wife's point of view too," Kamal concluded.

"In any case, we debated who to go to for a while. Dr. Nit Wit was out of the question for me. Eventually, she chose a family counseling clinic called *Building Bridges Counselors* not far from our house. I agreed for us to try something new."

"How did it go?" Adam asked.

"It was awful," Ray replied.

"What happened?" Adam and Kamal asked in unison.

Ray simply shook his head.

Part One: Section Three:
Marathon is a journey

"We did not make an immediate appointment to see the counselors at *Building Bridges Counselors*. We procrastinated for a while. Well, life gets in the way, and the controlled chaos in our lives continued. Our relationship remained in an uneasy cruise control with me trying hard not to ask her for it to avoid conflict and annoying her. Although, what happened was not my fault, but it was as if she was holding me responsible for it. So, when February came, I thought of doing something special for Valentine's day to patch things up."

"Sweet thinking. Hope you did something wonderful," Kamal stated.

"Well, that was my intention, but it also ended badly," Ray regretted.

"C'mon! What did you do?" Kamal inquired.

"In my stupid spontaneity again, I decided to give her a nice bouquet of 50 red roses and a box of exquisite Swiss chocolate. I bought her a heart-shaped ruby pendant necklace that was on sale at 20% off at *The Royal Jewelers* store on Woodlawn Avenue in Virginia. The necklace was very beautiful with ruby studs on gold," Ray explained with a smile.

"Nice!" Adam remarked.

"However, in my opinion, the card was the best gift of

them all. I designed the card myself by cutting cardboard into a heart shape, and I painted it. I glued some cuttings from designer magazines to add to its beauty. I wanted it to be original. Honestly, I wrote her a poem that I thought was a masterpiece. It took me two weeks to complete the card," Ray recalled with a sense of pride.

U are who U are

U are the center of my universe
U are the apple of my eyes
U are the desire of my heart
U are the joy of my life
U are the girl who rocks my boat
U are the babe who rings my bell
U are the chick who shakes my world

U are the p-a-s-s in my passion
U are the punch in my fruit punch
U are the juice in my orange juice
U are the sweet in my sweetener
U are the object of my objective
U are the subject of my affection
U are the beauty, I am the beau

U are my candy girl
U are the one I love
U are the one I crave
U are the lady for me

U are my love
U are my life
U are my dream
U are my fantasy
U are my reality

U have no idea how much U mean to me

I love you

"That is truly amazing! I expect her to be ecstatic. So, what happened?" Adam asked Ray.

"She accepted the gifts and read the card, but it wasn't with the excitement that I was expecting," Ray lamented.

"What did you mean? She did not appreciate it?" Adam sought clarification.

"If she appreciated it, she surely had a very poor way of showing it. I mean, her 'thank you' was half-witted. She accepted the flowers; she just looked at the pendant and put it down. She did not even try it on. She read the card, and her face just showed a faint smile. It did not reflect all the effort I put into it. It was a gross under-appreciation. I would have expected her to show some emotions, maybe a little scream in excitement and a speedy trip in front of the mirror to put the pendant on...and a hug and kiss perhaps," Ray recalled sounding disappointed.

"Maybe it was, you know, that she was pre-occupied in her thought. You wouldn't want her to fake an excitement," Adam expressed.

"Of course, I want her to be excited. Even it was fake! I will take that over her lackluster performance. I tried to hide my frustration. In the end, I asked her if she had anything for me. I was trying to bring her out of her shell. I was trying to get my baby back, you know make her lively again. Her reaction shocked me."

"What did she do?" Adam inquired.

"She stormed out of the house like someone on a dangerous vengeful mission. After about one hour, she came back with a nice belt and a card. I said a heartfelt 'thank you' to her which she simply waived off. When I read the content of the card, I did not know whether to be thankful that she did not hit me with the belt. It was as if, you know...as if what she wanted to do with the belt and she couldn't, she decided to do with her words," Ray explained.

"What did she write in the card?" Adam asked, being curious.

The fruits and veggies of life
You are also the apple of my eyes
You are the strawberry of my heart
You are the pear of my ears
You are the tulip of my hip
You are the plum of my bum
You are the cherry that makes me merry but
You are also the peanut that drives me nuts

Adam and Kamal wanted to laugh so bad, especially at her opinion that Ray is nuts and his nuts are driving her nuts. However, the matter is too serious, and they suppressed their laughter. This was no laughing matter.

"I was disappointed, and I let her know. I told her that if she was tired of being my wife, she should just say so. There is no point in tormenting me. She did not respond. That night she said *No, leave me alone* again. I mean it was totally nonsensical. Who says no to her husband on Valentine's day? Well, mine did." Ray asked a question and answered it himself.

Ray continued, "Apparently, worse things are yet to come. Her keeping me at arm's length increased. I got frustrated and became withdrawn. I leave home and return whenever I like. I stopped telling her my whereabouts. I did not play with the children. I just got exhausted being in the house. So, I started going to the gym more and more and tried to stay away from the house as much as I can. I mean, what is the purpose of coming home to a woman who keeps treating you badly? Unfortunately, I ran into a different problem in the gym."

"Really? What happened?" Kamal asked.

"It was as if I went from a hot frying pan into another, but hotter frying pan. I think the person who designed the sports bra should be prosecuted," Ray opined.

"For what crime?" Kamal asked.

"The chicks in the gym are always hot...wearing next to nothing," Ray explained.

"And you are always cold, having been put on ice by Desiree," Kamal surmised.

"What can I say? I mean, when you want the big bang, and you got a kiss instead with a promissory verbal note that says, 'Just hold on baby...I will be right back.' Only that the 'right back' means 48 hours later," Ray clarified, making air quotes while mentioning 'right back.'

"Well, every relationship can start very hot, but eventually all relationships cool down. The hope is that they don't dip into freezing, which unfortunately can be precocious," Kamal opined.

"I think Ray's marriage is at room temperature," Adam suggested.

"Absolutely not!" Ray snarled. "Desiree put our marriage in the freezer and occasionally brings it out to thaw a little bit."

"It is all about the temperature for men, but most ladies have no clue about the effect of their actions on their husbands," Kamal regretted.

"What do you mean?" Adam inquired.

Kamal responded, "Think about ladies as being a continuum of temperatures. The *hot* chick and her *hot* legs cool you down when you get hot, right?"

Ray and Adam nodded in agreement.

"Yeah. Okay. *Hot* ladies take care of hotness from guys. It is more like when firefighters use controlled burning in the forest to control wild forest fires," Kamal continued. "However, some ladies are warm. For those, let us just say, they are still there for you. Then there are those who are lukewarm or at room temperature. For those, we can agree that they are like the proverbial half-bread that is better than none. Unfortunately, a lot of wives are freezing cold, and they make you wonder why the world is against you," Kamal concluded.

Ray continued his tale of woes. "One Saturday morning, Desiree and I were yelling at each other in the presence of Lisa, who became quite disturbed, and started crying. I don't even remember what the bone of contention was, but I am pretty sure that Desiree was at fault."

"As always!" Kamal interjected with tongue in cheek.

Ray ignored him and continued. "Anyway, the sadness expressed by Lisa made us stop yelling at each other. Desiree picked the phone and called *Building Bridges Counselors* to make an appointment with a marriage counselor for us. Well, they are open on Saturdays too. I guess business is good for them, as many marriages are in chaos. On listening to the menu of options, we realized that they have a number of counselors, and prospective clients can choose a specific counselor they prefer. Desiree just selected the first lady counselor whose name was mentioned in the prompt since we did not know any of them and we had no references. Honestly, I would have preferred Mama wise, because she is truly wise and experienced. In addition, her counseling session was free! On the other hand, *Building Bridges Counselors* charge fees per hour. I imagined that their clients would have to talk quickly in order to get their money's worth of counseling. We got a late afternoon appointment for that Monday."

Ray paused and chuckled, making Kamal and Adam look at each other, wondering what was amiss.

"So?" Kamal asked, urging Ray to continue.

"When we got to *Building Bridges Counselors*, we waited for our turn in the large beautifully designed reception area with beautiful flowery curtains. The curtains were drawn to expose a well-trimmed luscious green lawn outside. The amazing glow of the gradually fading sun cast light into the room. The reception area was well decorated with plastic flowers in the recesses and had a high cathedral ceiling. The ceiling was decorated with paintings and ceiling fans with exquisite designs, but the blades were not moving because the fans were not turned on. The wallpaper was beautiful, and some paintings of exotic places like The Eifel Tower, Mount Rushmore, and the Great Wall of China hung in strategic places on the walls. The room was serene and comforting with soft cushioned sofa and recliners. The floor was covered in a crimson red carpet with an ancient design, giving it an elegance that would take your breath away. The atmosphere was very conducive and will make you feel that you are in the right place to solve all your marital problems. I could immediately sense that I was going to leave there broke."

Kamal chuckled.

"I was surprised to see many couples in the waiting area when we got there. Some were holding hands while other couples sat away from each other. Most of the men occupied their time by watching the television while the women were mainly binge-reading numerous magazines dealing with fashion and styles. Later, the receptionist called us and obtained our information, including my credit card number for us to pay out-of-pocket for their services since marital counseling was not covered by my private health insurance."

Ray paused and looked at Adam and asked, "Why is it that private health insurance companies and even Medicare and Medicaid do not fully cover marital counseling?"

Adam shrugged his shoulders and opened his hands in an 'I don't know' gesture.

Ray continued, "Shouldn't they recognize that the greatest mental health derangement issues start in the home, and solving marital disputes through helping couples will save them more money in psychotherapy for all the family members and prevent psychiatric illness among the children?"

Adam nodded in agreement.

"In any case, I think marital counseling should be fully covered by all health insurance companies, including Medicare and Medicaid. Anyway, soon afterward, the receptionist ushered us into a beautiful consultation room with plastic flowers on the table, and boxes of brightly colored serviettes were also on the table. I guess they put them there in case we want to cry or something."

"Our randomly selected marriage counselor, Alyssa DeRogue, turned out to be a recent college graduate. We did not ask her how old she was, but I am absolutely sure that she couldn't be more than twenty-three years old. She still had braces in her mouth!"

Adam and Kamal chuckled.

"When she walked in with a clipboard in her hand to verify our identities, we initially thought she was another receptionist, maybe just back from her bathroom break. When she introduced herself as our marital counselor, Desiree and I looked at each other saying, 'OH NO!' without uttering a word."

"Alyssa realized it. I guess she has gotten that reaction before. So, she smiled and said, "I am guessing that you think I should be older. However, we are here to talk about you, not about me. So, it is still your show.""

"What did you guys say?" Adam inquired.

"Well, there was nothing to say. We chose her and we were already there, and my credit card meter had started running for our hour-long consultation. We might as well start talking, and talking fast."

All three friends broke into hysterical laughter.

"Well, it was too late to leave. We resigned to our fate that a lady who is almost young enough to be our daughter is going to be telling us what to do to stay married or be happily married. It was quite a kick in the shin considering that the counselor is probably not married herself. After the introduction, she set the grounds rules which included talking to her only except when she permits us to look at each other and talk directly to each other, like when she told us to look at each other and say 'I love you' stuff. She started by asking us if our goal, after the therapy session, is to go home bitter or better?"

"Interesting question," Kamal remarked.

"She was not bad at all in her approach. I guess old age, maturity, and experience do have their perks but being young

‖‖‖‖‖‖‖‖‖‖‖‖‖‖‖‖‖‖‖

0004389786 4

**Sell your books at
sellbackyourBook.com!**
Go to sellbackyourBook.com
and get an instant price
quote. We even pay the
shipping - see what your old
books are worth today!

Inspected By: Karina_Lopez

is not necessarily a disadvantage, especially in a matter concerning love and relationship which has no defined formula for success," Ray suggested.

Adam cleared his throat in jest and put his right hand behind his right ear and faced Ray. Then he remarked, "Could you please say that again so that deaf old people of the world who feel that wisdom and blissful marriage is a function of age can hear you?"

Kamal knew that Adam was retaliating with his own jab regarding his preference for Nora over Aneida, but he chose to ignore Adam too. He simply mused to himself that Adam is too blinded by an infatuation with Nora to see the reality of his situation.

Ray continued, "Anyway, she gave each of us a pen and plain sheet of paper and asked Desiree to write her top three reasons why a man marries a woman and asked me to write my top three reasons why a woman marries a man. We did and gave the sheets of paper to her. While she was looking at our responses, Desiree spoke in a loud voice, "We wouldn't be here if not for my 'perfect' husband," she said, making air quotes while saying 'perfect.'

Ray retorted immediately saying, "We wouldn't be here if not for my 'flawless' wife," making his own air quotes too while saying 'flawless.' He then continued, "My wife maltreats me all the time. She is mean. She is the only honey in the world that is bitter."

He then faced Desiree, breaking the rule set by the counselor, and remarked, "Honey, why are you so bitter to me?"

Desiree would not let him get away with his non-salutary comment. No way! She responded immediately.

"Oh yeah! My husband calls himself 'alpha!'" She exclaimed, making air quotes again while saying 'alpha.' She then faced Ray and remarked, "Alpha, why are you so beta?"

Ray faced the counselor again and remarked, "My wife is stone cold. She is frozen."

He then faced Desiree and remarked, "Why are you so frigid?"

No sooner than Ray finished his statement when Desiree responded while facing the counselor saying, "My husband is rigid."

At this point, Alyssa chuckled, making Ray and Desiree pause with surprise. Alyssa continued, "You guys are super cool for each other. I mean, your love—it's lit. Awesome! Totally legit! It's like…you guys are so imperfect, but you are, literarily, so seriously perfect for each other. I mean, yours is truly a match made in heaven. I am so seriously not kidding. A *rigid* husband is accusing his *frigid* wife of being stone cold. Sounds so awesomely poetic!"

She immediately proceeded to complete her reading of the couple's response to the top three reasons why a man marries a woman and vice versa.

Ray and Desiree were shocked that this lady, who is almost young enough to be their child, is counseling them and mocking them at the same time. However, before they could utter a word, she spoke again, having completed her review of their answers. "You guys are literarily…I mean…very perfect for each other. You have a lot in common. It's like, as if you are identical twins, or something like that." There was an uncanny excitement in her voice.

Ray continued that he felt ashamed of hearing Alyssa's comments. This is a lady who most likely young enough to be his daughter, and she is going to advise him about his relationship with his wife. It was so annoying. He was still lost in thought when Alyssa spoke again she remarked, "In my few years of being part of marital counseling sessions, I have literarily never seen this. You guys actually agree with each other." Her voice rose to excitement again.

"We were puzzled again as per what she meant," Ray recalled. "Subsequently, she gave my note to Desiree and gave her note to me to read. It was interesting and strange."

"What happened?" Adam inquired.

"For her top 3 reasons why a man marries a woman, Desiree wrote:

1. The need for an unpaid maid.
2. The need to remain like a baby while being an adult.
3. The need to have somebody to annoy on a regular basis.

For my top three reasons why a woman marries a man, I had written:

1. The need for a human ATM.
2. The need for somebody to fertilize her eggs.
3. The need to have somebody to annoy on a regular basis."

Adam and Kamal laughed. "Now, I see why she was excited," Kamal remarked.

"Anyway, Alyssa spoke with a great authority, not minding the fact that myself and Desiree in front of her are old enough to be her uncle and aunt or even her parents."

"You guys have serious problems, but you are perfect for each other! Wow! In my six months of doing this marriage counseling thing by myself, this is the first time a couple with serious problems actually wrote the truth about why they got married. I must give it to you guys. Absolutely, yours was a match made in heaven. No doubt, I was going to say hell, but I realized that only heaven can put something this amazing together."

Ray and Desiree looked at each other and then at the counselor wondering what was wrong with this young woman, but they remained quiet. Then she passed her comments on what each of them wrote as per the reasons why they got married. "If we are to draw a Venn diagram, you guys will have a perfect overlap on the main reason why you got married. It is really the root of your problems, and both of you literarily put it as number three, without looking at the notes of the other partner. It was like, you literarily wanted somebody to annoy on a regular basis, and you guys have each other to do just that! Bravo! The only thing that I am not sure of is why you married each other for that? I mean, like, rather than love or money or status or beauty or anything else which is more common for normal people."

Ray interpreted Alyssa's statement to mean that they were an abnormal couple, but before he could respond, Desiree spoke, "We were just being sarcastic."

"Sarcastic, but truthful," remarked Alyssa.

Desiree got up sharply and held Ray's right hand to pull him from his chair and said, "Let's go. This counselor does not know what she is talking about."

Ray remarked, "On the contrary, I think she is right. We were both thinking of not getting hurt or the hurt we feel, that we did not notice the hurt the other partner feels."

He then stood up and held Desiree's hand while looking at her and said, "Baby, why are you mad at me all the time? What did I do to you?"

Desiree sighed and lowered her head, but she did not speak. She had tear laden eyes but fought it. It was obvious that something was bothering her, but she still refused to speak.

Ray let go of her hand and faced Alyssa. "You see my point."

Alyssa motioned for both of them to sit down for the therapy session to continue. They sat down. She then encouraged Desiree to speak. After some minutes of awkward silence, Desiree spoke, fighting her tears again.

"Ray, it is not you. It is me."

"Baby, that is what people say when they want to break up if they don't want the other party to feel too bad," Ray responded.

"Unfortunately, Desiree did not elaborate further. Soon afterward, the counseling session was over. Alyssa said she looked forward to seeing us the following week. However, after a moment of silence, while driving home, Desiree looked at me and asked, 'Did you really think that I married you because I needed somebody to be annoying on a regular basis?' I replied, 'I thought that was what you wrote down too?' After this exchange, we stayed quiet for the rest of the journey home. Her behavior at home was better for a short time, though, but we never went back for further therapy sessions despite my appeal to her," Ray lamented.

"How many sessions did the therapist recommend?" Adam asked Ray.

"Alyssa had recommended a session per week for three months, and we could extend it after reassessment of our progress," Ray replied.

"But you guys never went back?" Adam sought clarification.

"You are correct. Desiree did not want us to go back. There was no point in me going back by myself and spending money unnecessarily. I did not need therapy. She is the one who needed therapy, but she did not want to go."

> **Author's note:** Is there something Ray could have done to get Desiree to attend more sessions? Would it have been better for Ray to continue going for the counseling session by himself if Desiree continues to refuse to attend?

Ray took a sip of his drink and continued. "One day at the gym, one of the guys, Paolo mentioned that he wanted to run in the forthcoming Marine Corps Marathon. Some of the guys had run it before, but I never thought of running a marathon. I don't even run to my car. The only time I run is while trying to catch the elevator. Somehow, I thought it was a great idea. I registered for the marathon when registration started. Paolo advised me to run at least three times a week. I started with my treadmill at home and at the gym. When I got to run five miles on the treadmill, Paolo advised running on the street or running trail, as it was different from running in place with the belt moving you forward while on a treadmill. Initially, I tried running around our street, but I became shy. I mean, everybody was greeting me. I could see it on their faces that they were saying to themselves, 'You should have been doing this all along.' I later saw some fashionably slim guys on bikes trying to do their own version of *Tour de France* in the neighborhood. I was struggling to climb a small hill at that time. It really took a lot of energy. When I got to the top of the hill, they gave me a round of applause. They had been waiting for their compatriots, but I did not realize that they had been watching me struggle up the hill. The applause was very encouraging, but it was a testament that I needed a lot more encouragement. The day I started running on the trail was really a day to remember."

"What happened?" Kamal inquired.

"The people at the trail were very friendly. I guess it was not very common for them to see a guy who is heavy in the middle coming to run on the trail. I said to myself that I was going to run a half marathon the first day."

"That was awesome. Did you accomplish it?" Adam asked with some excitement.

"Are you kidding me?" Ray asked rhetorically. After I ran about half a mile it was as if I was having a heart attack. So, I slowed down a bit. It was a lot tougher to run on the ground than to run on a treadmill. I saw a rest area for those who were members of the Anacostia Running club. Some of their members were beginning their ten-mile run. I thought it was a great idea to join them stride for the 5-miles they would run towards the east, and when they turn back, I would just continue to complete my target running goal. You can tell that these guys and gals run a lot. I matched them stride for stride the first thirty seconds or so. I really tried to keep up with them, but after about two minutes of running or so, these runners were so far away I couldn't even see any of them."

Adam and Kamal chuckled.

Ray ignored them and continued. "So, I started pacing

myself. Suddenly, a young man passed me. I dismissed it. After all, he is a young man. If I were his age, I would have run faster too. I was still analyzing this when a young lady zoomed past me. I was shocked to see how fast she ran. It bruised my manly ego a bit, but I was quick to dismiss her accomplishment. I told myself that I was still warming up; otherwise, there is no way a lady would have overtaken me. After a few minutes, an older gentleman passed me. When I realized that all his hair was gray, I felt it was ridiculous to be beaten by an old man. So, I increased my speed. I tried catching up with him, but I couldn't. So, I let him go, you know, rationalizing that he must have been running all his life. I made up my mind that I would not let any older lady pass me. I was thinking about this and psyching myself up when three ladies passed by me."

Adam and Kamal looked at each other and laughed.

Ray continued, "That was not the painful part."

"What happened?" inquired Kamal.

"These ladies were talking about a guy at work, and they were laughing and talking while I was breathless. It was disappointing. They passed by me as if I wasn't even there. After they left, I tried to increase my speed, but I could not go faster. Out of the blue, an old woman passed me while she was barely running. I felt so ashamed that I increased my speed and I overtook her. After a few minutes, she passed me again. I increased my speed and I caught up with her and overtook her again, but a few minutes later, she overtook me again. At that point, I let her go because I did not want her to have a heart attack."

"Yeah, right!" Adam remarked.

"You couldn't keep up with an old woman?" Kamal questioned.

"You can say whatever you want. I made up my mind and I made a rule which I have kept and chiseled in stone since then."

"And what would that be?" Kamal inquired.

"I made up my mind that when I am running, nobody who is walking would overtake me. I have kept this rule since then," Ray complimented himself.

"You are really crazy. Do you really think the bar you set is low enough?" Kamal asked Ray.

"It is not just low, it is completely underground," Adam commented.

Ray ignored the comments of his buddies and continued, "After running for almost an hour, I saw a mile marker ahead on a small elevation on the trail. I ran quickly to it, making my own impression of Sylvester Stallone as Rocky on the steps of the Philadelphia Museum of Art. I truly felt a sense of accomplishment when I realized that I had run three miles. I felt great despite the pain I felt in both shoulders, my right rib cage, my thighs, my calves, and my feet. Then I became sad."

"What happened?" Adam questioned.

"It suddenly dawned on me that I have nothing left in my energy tank to go an additional three and a half miles further before turning back, in order to make a half marathon. The worst part was that I still had to go an additional three miles back to where I started to get back to my car and go home."

Adam and Kamal started laughing.

"It was not funny, brother! I really wished I could take a taxicab back to the starting point at the trail rest station where I parked. Unfortunately, cars do not go on the trail. Nonetheless, it would take quite a walk to get to the road in the first place. I seriously contemplated stopping one of the guys on bikes and ask to hitchhike back to where my car was. I started walking back when a big dude joined the trail close to a neighborhood. He was very cheerful. He looked at me and remarked, "You looked very tired. Is this your first time here at the trail?"

"I confirmed it for him, and he smiled and said congratulations and extended his hand. I shook his hand as he told me that his name is Heavy B," Ray recalled.

"Heavy B?" Adam queried.

"Yeah! He said that is what he goes by. His real name is Bernard. I introduced myself to him too, and we started walking and talking. He told me that he has been living in the neighborhood for about ten years and he comes to walk about six miles three times a week for about a year. If you look at the guy's size, you will find it hard to believe. However, he walked really fast, and I had to keep up while talking to him. He told me that he had lost fifty pounds in the previous year. That was impressive. He told me that he reduced his portion sizes. He eats more vegetables and has increased his physical activities. It was really encouraging to listen to him discuss his challenges and how he has tackled the problems head-on. It was quite inspirational for me. At that point, I had only lost five pounds out of my goal of twenty-five pounds. Even my wife called my weight loss 'due to just skipping a breakfast' making air quotes. It is so difficult to lose weight. Prevention is truly better than cure when it comes to maintaining body weight. Unfortunately, Desiree has not been encouraging at all. Well, sometimes I don't listen to her, either."

"What did you mean?" Kamal inquired.

"Sometimes, she is too controlling and her so-called 'words of encouragement' can be quite condescending," Ray explained while making air quote. "However, after three months of going to the gym regularly, I looked at myself shirtless in front of the mirror while combing my hair and thought, *Wow!* I saw an amazing transformation."

"Your muscles reappeared?" Adam asked in jest.

Ray shook his head and said, "Well, let's just say, I knew James Brown was thinking of me."

So good
I am good, really good
I look good, so good
I feel good, too good
I smell good, very good
Try me, baby, try me.

Ray took a sip of his drink and continued, "I entered for the marathon and continued my training. This also helps me get out of the house too. There were many times that I felt discouraged about running, but Paolo and Heavy B kept encouraging me. Later, Heavy B suggested that I tell a lot of people about my plan to run the marathon. That way, it will be more difficult to chicken out of it. I did just that, but many people thought that I was crazy, and their comments were not encouraging at all. The most distasteful comment was from one of my colleagues who suggested that my desire to run the marathon was a form of a midlife crisis."

"Oh, I see. They were not encouraging," Kamal remarked.

"No, I thought they felt they were being funny. I just ignored them and was more committed to proving them wrong. The initial fun was actually at the marathon party at the Stadium Armory near JFK stadium in Washington DC when we collected our bibs, tags, and the timer along with the T-shirts we purchased at the time of registration. After I got my package, a guy standing next to me asked me if I was collecting it for someone else. I replied that it was mine. Then he asked me if I was running the marathon and I replied in the affirmative, but I could see the surprise on his face. Then it dawned on me that he probably did not think that I fit the profile of a marathon runner in his head. I thought to myself that people with prejudice need to understand that heavy set people can move too, even if it is slowly."

Kamal nodded in agreement and inquired, "So what happened on the day of the marathon?"

"It was a cold Sunday morning in October. The Metro subway train station started running early to accommodate the big event, and the parking in the Metro was free. The Marine Corps Marathon was a lot of fun. Getting to the start line itself felt like walking a baby marathon by itself. It was a long walk from the Metro train station, pass the security checkpoints before reaching the runners' village. This assembly point had several portable toilets and UPS trucks to help move personal items to the end of the race. The race started with artillery fire from a howitzer. The runners line up based on their expected finish time. I was at the back. My goal was finishing the race. I did not think that I stand a chance to win it...well, except if everybody were to just stand in place."

Adam and Kamal chuckled.

Ray continued with his Marathon tale, "I started the race pacing myself between 10 and 11 minutes per mile. My initial goal was to 'beat the bridge' by getting to 20 miles of the race within 5 hours. Men! I was ecstatic when I made it there on time. I did a lot of walking for the rest of the race. I mean, everywhere hurts. There were lots of people cheering on their family members and anybody that looked tired. So, you can guess that a lot of people were lying to me."

"What did you mean by that? I thought you said that they were cheering you guys on," Kamal queried.

"Of course, they were cheering us on while lying to us. For example, somebody sounded excited about seeing that I was so tired at mile marker sixteen. She yelled, "You are almost there!"

Kamal chuckled.

"I know. What is almost there? I still had ten long miles to go," Ray explained and started laughing. "It was a lot of fun. I must tell you. Many runners had messages on their apparel honoring family members, especially deceased soldiers. Others wore tee shirts with funny messages on their backs like 'If you can read this, I am ahead of you,' 'Run like you stole something,' 'Laugh if you want, I am still moving,' and 'At this pace, I will cross the finish line before sunset.' There were people wearing costumes of superheroes from comics, and a guy was juggling stuff while running. The disappointing part was that the guy juggling stuff was still faster than me."

Adam remarked, "Your finishing the race is what matters. Most human beings will never run a marathon in their lifetime."

"You are quite right. Crossing the finish line brought indescribable joy to me. When I saw the finish line, I mustered all the remaining energy I had to run up the small elevation. The marines at the finish line were shouting congratulations. The best part was when they put my medal around my neck like they do in the award ceremony in the Olympics. I bit the edge of my medal while my picture was taken as part of the official celebration. I felt the joy of true accomplishment."

"Outstanding! How long did it take you to complete the marathon?" Adam inquired.

"I am not telling you," Ray replied.

"C'mon! I am just curious."

"Okay. I finished it in six hours and thirty minutes."

"Six hours?" Adam sounded surprised.

"Are you kidding me? I was not the finisher."

"What did you mean?" Adam sought clarification. "I thought you said you finished the run."

"Yes, I did. The finisher is the last person to finish the race officially. I was ahead of some people. I did not come last in the race. Show some respect!"

The three men started laughing.

Yes. Ray survived the Marine Corps Marathon. Semper Fi.

"Desiree and the children were very happy when I got home with my medal. I guess they were surprised too. I tried to get more involved in 'home affairs,' and I was going to the gym regularly. Things got a little better until I traveled for a summit in Vienna, Austria for a couple of weeks. I did not realize that Desiree was busy forgetting to take her birth control pills."

Ray paused, sighed, and in a reserved tone declared to his friends, "Well, Desiree is pregnant."

"What! I mean, wow!" Adam quickly caught himself. "You guys are expecting another baby?"

"Yes," Ray affirmed, resigning to fate.

"Should I say congratulations or sorry?" Adam asked him.

"C'mon! It is always...em...congratulations!" Kamal interjected.

After a moment of awkward silence, Ray continued. "It was a rude shock to me," as he recalled the conversation between him and Desiree regarding this pregnancy for which they were totally unprepared.

"I am late," Desiree informed Ray while he was watching a rerun of an exciting sitcom.

"You are always late," Ray responded, dismissing the conversation while picking up the TV remote control and increasing the volume.

In a stern voice, Desiree remarked, "I am serious." She picked the remote control and switched the TV off; the first time ever that she switched off the TV while Ray was watching it.

Ray was shocked as he has never seen Desiree in such a perplexed defeated mood before. He wanted to get angry with her for switching off the TV, but he couldn't. Something really catastrophic must have happened.

"I am late," Desiree repeated her statement while fighting her tears.

Ray sat up from the couch looking puzzled. "Late for what?" he asked.

Desiree's silence was deafening.

Ray froze. He realized the gravity of what his wife was

telling him. Finally, he mustered the courage to put his thought into words. "No, it cannot be."

She walked to the bathroom, took her pregnancy test kit, and brought the kit for Ray to interpret for himself. Ray did not bother to collect it from her. It must be true. It has to be true. It can only be true. It is the consequence of this truth that is making him hope that it is not true. The reality that just paid him a permanent visit was making him rush into self-deceit and baseless denial of the possibility of his wife being pregnant. After all, this was no immaculate conception, but an ejaculate conception. He just thought that they were done in that department. Their youngest child, Lisa, is already nine years old. This positive pregnancy test represented a return to diapers, waking up at odd hours of the night to feed a parasite, singing an unending lullaby to pacify a pest, attending to the never-ending need of a bloodsucker or struggling to get free from a leech, just to have a simple two hours of peace and quiet. The absolutely worst part is the *no-no leave me alone* that will constantly rain on him till thy kingdom comes and goes. This was way too much for Ray, and he yelled, "I can't believe it! What happened? How did it happen?" He asked many questions without waiting for an answer. He did not even notice that Desiree was sobbing.

With a broken voice in between desperate attempts to fight her tears, Desiree mustered, "I forgot my pills when you traveled."

"Why did you not say something when I got back? Why? Why? Why did you do this to me?" Ray asked without sympathy.

"Excuse me!" Desiree snarled at him. "I did something to you? Or did you mean the other way around? Are you the one to carry the pregnancy? Are you the one that will be having nausea and vomiting? Are you the one who is going to lose shape even more? Are you the one to endure sleepless nights and not be able to find a comfortable position to sleep soundly? Tell me, Ray, are you the one who will be taking pills every day, and will try to bear the pain of labor while trying not to make a mess of yourself? Are your nipples going to be charred and sore from breastfeeding? Are you the one to constantly wake up every two hours to attend to the needs of a tiny baby that cannot fend for himself or herself?"

Desiree continued on and on until Ray could no longer stand her rhetorical questions.

"Stop it, Desiree!" Ray shouted while raising his hands. "You really think that you are the only one who goes through all those challenges that you mentioned? Did you ever ask yourself how things are with me to see you go through all those challenges? Do you really think fathers go tap dancing enjoying themselves when their wives are in labor or are you just saying those things because you have no understanding that a husband who loves his wife will be in a worse state than you undergoing the labor because a part of him will constantly feel guilty of putting you through it? The most unbearable part is that a man has absolutely no control over the outcome and cannot even help his wife in alleviating the challenges and difficulties that she is facing. That is very tough on most men. They just don't want to talk about it. Did you ever ask yourself why men sometimes do not want to have children anymore after the first child? Believe me, it is not just because they do not want a competitor for the attention of their wives."

Ray then left the living room, went to the bedroom to get his shirt, and decided to go for a walk to clear his head. As he got outside, he saw their neighbor whose pregnancy seems to have reached term as she struggled to get into her car, a compact four-door sedan. Ray waved at her, and she waved back as she forced a smile. Observing his neighbor's ordeal made his heart jump into his mouth as the reality of what is about to come dawned on him.

Author's note: To our female readers, if you have given birth previously, ask your spouse what his experience was when you were going through the throes of pregnancy and delivery. I am quite sure that this interesting conversation may give you a different perspective.

"Desiree has been cranky ever since," Ray continued. "Although she wasn't as sick this time around and had not been vomiting, she seemed to have lost interest in everything. I guess pregnancy is a lot harder on women who have advanced in age. Being pregnant with a fifth child at thirty-eight years of age was definitely not on her to-do list."

"How is she holding up?" Adam asked with a lot of concern. "So-so! Maturity in age is not an advantage when it comes to pregnancy. Well, she is trying to accept fate. The pregnancy is progressing but still a long way to go," Ray responded. "I tried to cheer her up last weekend and it ended in a disaster. I will never be spontaneous again."

"What happened?" asked Kamal. Ray simply shook his head and repeated his statement, "I will never be spontaneous again."

"C'mon, man! What happened?" Kamal repeated his question. Ray bellowed a heavy sigh and narrated his misadventure while trying to cheer up his distraught pregnant wife.

I arranged with my mother-in-law to kindly take care of our children while I take Desiree out on a 'me and you only' getaway surprise. She kept asking me what the surprise was, but I did not tell her emphasizing to her that it will ruin the surprise. We drove to Baltimore and left the children with Nana, as we fondly call her. I then drove her to the interstate section terminal of *Busline*. She followed me with a lot of reluctance as we traversed the terminal to find our bus. When I informed her to board the bus bound for New York with me, Desiree was surprised, but not in a good way. I should have known that it was a disaster waiting to happen," Ray lamented.

"I don't get it. What did she do?" Kamal inquired. "Desiree queried the rationale for going to New York with very sharp criticism in her tone. I then informed her that I wanted to take her down the memory lane to the Convention Center in the University of Brooklyn where it all started, as a way of celebrating our relationship, hoping it would bring her some smiles and joy."

Your effect on me

I think about you
And I am beaming with smiles
I look at you
And I develop goosebumps
I hear your voice
And I hear the melody of love
I smell your fragrance
And my heart gallops away
I talk to you
And I get elated to cloud nine
I hold your hand
And I am out of this world!
I love you

"Why not fly instead of a long bus ride?" Desiree asked with a reservation while boarding the bus.

"We will get there too quickly," Ray replied.

"Why not the high-speed train?" Desiree questioned again.

"Because it is high-speed and we will also get there too soon," Ray responded.

"Why didn't we drive then if you want us to go slowly?" Desiree reasoned with a stern voice.

"I am sure that you would have wanted us to bring the kids with us, but this is just for you and me. It is not just about the destination; it is about the journey itself. It is not just about the trip; it is about getting to spend quality time with you alone," Ray explained.

Desiree shook her head in disbelief rather than in excitement. She took her seat next to the window, looking out at no scenery in particular. In contrast, Ray was excited and held her right hand saying to her, "Today, I have you for myself for at least ten hours." This made Desiree sigh while shaking her head. "Is this a surprise? What a stupid surprise," she mused to herself.

Ray shook his head and declared to his friend, "I am done with being spontaneous. The trip concept was good to me, but the implementation was a disaster. Desiree was miserable throughout. On our way to New York, she complained about people putting their bags on seats, overhead storage with soft ropes as barriers rather than enclosed plastics like obtained in airplanes and being afraid that the luggage may fall on people sitting. She complained about other passengers talking loudly on the phone."

"Sounds bad," Adam opined.

"That is not the worst part," Ray continued.

"Really?" Adam questioned.

Ray mused and said, "Desiree's experience with the bathroom was the worst. It was as if she was peeing every 20 minutes. She hated the bathroom on the bus. She complained that the bathroom was not clean enough, and it ran out of toilet paper. It was just fortuitous that she had a bathroom tissue in her bag, which she had brought along for the kids when we left home. When we reached the bus terminal in New York about 3 hours later, she rushed into the bathroom at the station only to find it partially flooded. She was livid. I was dumbfounded, but I still wanted to salvage whatever I could of the ruined surprise trip. I apologized to her and asked that we go on campus to where we met at the conference center at the University of Brooklyn. She agreed, but it was obvious that she was not happy at all. Unfortunately, when we got to the conference hall, it was locked for repairs, as it experienced some flooding from a broken water main two days previously and we could not enter the building. It was beyond a disappointment."

"Oh, God!" Kamal exclaimed.

"I did not know what to say other than to apologize again. She wanted to yell at me, but I think she couldn't find the strength or composure to do so without attracting too much unwanted attention. So, she simply kept quiet and ignored me. I then suggested that we could go to the original site for the feeding the homeless program where she organized the students like a Field Marshall, but she was not having any of it. She just wanted us to leave for home immediately."

"So sorry for your plight," Adam expressed.

"Well, what can I say? On the one hand, I understand her frustration. However, on the other hand, I could not understand why she did not see my efforts as being laudable. I went through all this to cheer her up. Granted, it did not go as planned, but c'mon! She shouldn't treat me as if I committed a crime!" Ray lamented. "Unfortunately, I was very frustrated by her frustration. I tried to see if I could book a one-way flight for us to Baltimore Washington International Airport right away. As fate would have it on this mighty day, there was no available flight for two people, and it would not make sense for me to book a flight only for her. I later found an available flight from Larguadia Airport to Reagan National Airport in Washington DC, but it was set to leave 6 hours later. This would have meant that we would have reached Baltimore by our scheduled bus trip by *Busline* before the plane touched down in DC, and we would still have to travel to Baltimore to pick up our vehicle, then get the kids. So, it was not worth pursuing. So, we headed back to *Busline* terminal in agony to await our return trip back to Baltimore."

"I am so sorry for your plight," Adam repeated.

"Thank you, my friend. I guess it is one of those things. As men, we do suffer a lot for our families, especially our wives. We work hard and put up with a lot of nonsense at work because we want to provide for them, care for them, make sure that they are okay, et cetera, but it appears that nobody understands this. Maybe it is just that they don't care that we do struggle a lot and work very hard for our families. Certainly, they do not give us any credit for trying. I mean, the return trip was beyond cold. After some people left the bus, Desiree went to seat somewhere else away from me on the other side of the bus.

"Maybe she wanted to be closer to the bathroom," Kamal tried to reason.

"Absolutely not!" came the sharp response from Ray. "She

sat in the empty seat in front. So, it was not that she wanted to be close to the bathroom. She obviously just wanted to be away from me. She did everything she could to avoid making eye contact with me. The few times she walked past my seat to the bathroom, I could see suppressed disappointment in her eyes, and I could feel pent up anger in her strides. It was as if I did something to hurt her deliberately."

Adam put his hand on Ray's left shoulder to sympathize and reassure him. Ray sighed and continued his lamentation. "How am I supposed to know that women pee a lot during pregnancy? I didn't dirty the toilet on the bus nor flooded the bathroom in the bus terminal in New York. I certainly didn't break the water pipe in the conference center at the University of Brooklyn and shut down the building. However, I am guilty of organizing a surprise trip that ended up in a disaster. She was really mad at me for putting her through this ordeal. I mean...we did not have any meaningful conversation at all in the eleven hours that we were together alone before we picked the children up from Nana. Desiree was not interested in talking to me at all. She just starred out of the window almost throughout the trip to New York, and she behaved as if she did not know who I was when we were coming back from New York. I was really angry in the end that when we got home, I was forced to ask her, 'What did I do to you that made you hate me so much?'"

"So? Did she tell you what was bothering her?" Adam inquired.

"No. She simply dismissed my question with 'I don't hate you' and walked away to attend to her kids."

"Hmm! I don't know what to say," Adam expressed.

"Well, there is nothing to say. Nothing needs to be said, except that I will never be spontaneous again! I really mean it. I will never be spontaneous again. Seriously, I will never be spontaneous again!" Ray concluded.

"Hopefully, as she feels better with the pregnancy, things will be better," Adam tried to be optimistic.

"I doubt it," Ray countered. "I seriously doubt it. I think, in the end, something has got to give. I vividly recalled asking her the following day, 'What exactly are you looking for that is making you treat me badly this way?'"

"And what was her response?" Adam inquired.

"She just gave me a blank look and did not answer me," Ray recalled. "I think she is very tired of being in my world."

At this, Kamal responded, "Don't let us jump so deep into conclusions. Let us take it to be hormonal issues surrounding pregnancy."

"But she has always been nasty to me, even when she was not pregnant," Ray countered.

"I know, but she still has female hormones, you know... em...em...even when she was not pregnant. They only increased during pregnancy," Kamal interjected.

"Did you mean I should be looking forward to her menopause, for her hormones to normalize and she becomes normal?" Ray inquired.

"Hormones don't 'normalize' at menopause," Adam interjected while making air quotes on mentioning normalize. "Rather, they actually decrease."

"Well, my point is that we make a lot of bogus excuses for ladies when they do not act right, blaming everything on hormones. We have hormones too. We have our male hormones too. You don't see or hear anybody giving men excuses for misbehaving, using male hormones as the 'not at fault excuse,' do you?" Ray asked while making air quotes while saying 'not at fault.'

Kamal and Adam nodded in agreement.

Ray continued. "Speaking of menopause, isn't that when they get hot flashes?"

"Hot flushes," Kamal corrected Ray.

"It is hot flashes, not hot flushes," Ray reiterated.

"I am pretty sure it is hot flushes, right doc?" Kamal restated his position while looking at Adam for the final verdict.

"Well, they are actually called *hot flashes,* but it is *flushing* due to decreased estradiol hormone level," Adam tried to clarify.

"So, it is flushing causing flashes," Kamal sought further clarification.

"Yes, I guess you could put it that way," Adam replied.

"Exactly my point—that everything about women is very

confusing. It is flushing, but it is flashing! Is flushing not when you increase blood to the body, causing heat and redness, but you said that they have reduced hormones making women drive men crazy?" Ray asked Adam.

"I did not say that they drive men crazy," Adam clarified.

"But they do, and you know that," Ray concluded. He then faced Kamal pointing at him and remarked, "Now, this genius here wants me to assume that Desiree will be a better wife when she is having hot flashes."

"C'mon, Ray! Chill. I am only saying that I expect things to get better over time with Desiree." Kamal explained.

"I am not being pessimistic, but I do not think all these behaviors or misbehaviors are due to hormonal factors at all. I think we are just rationalizing their behaviors to make us feel better. Even women will accuse you of sexism if you try to justify anything untoward regarding them using their hormones or menstrual cycles as excuses. All this premenstrual stuff is not looked upon kindly by women when they feel discriminated against. I am sure that a good woman is a good woman, whether she is pre or post-menopausal. After all, Bonita is a woman too, and she has hormones, right?" Ray asked Kamal.

"Yes," Kamal replied.

"But her hormones are not making her treat you badly, right?" Ray pressed on.

"I guess you are right," Kamal submitted.

"In any case, one thing that I am sure of is that I will never be spontaneous again. Never again. I will never be spontaneous again. I am through with been spontaneous trying to reach Desiree. I am going to resign to fate and take it as it comes. I will never be spontaneous again."

Adam and Kamal looked at each other and shrugged their shoulders. The pain and despondence in Ray's voice were palpable and understandable.

After a few minutes of silence with the three friends in pensive moods, Ray spoke again in lamentation. "I have done a lot of stuff trying to woo Desiree or try to make her happy both before and after our marriage, including stupid stuff that I later regretted."

"Like what?" Kamal interjected.

"There was this day in college that we attended a student gathering with lots of festivities in the campus quadrangle. Everybody was having fun. I do not remember what the occasion was anymore, but it was a fun-filled atmosphere. There were grills, hamburgers, and music everywhere. However, Desiree was in a pensive mood for an unknown reason. I tried to cheer her up, but she was not feeling it at all. She wanted to leave, but I didn't want to leave yet."

"Let me guess," Kamal interjected. "You reached a compromise, and you left," Kamal suggested with tongue in cheek while laughing and making air quotes on saying 'compromise.'

"No. We had to leave. I mean, I needed to leave," Ray recalled.

"Wait! What happened?" Kamal asked, sounding puzzled at the unexpected twist in the story.

"Well," Ray continued. "I wanted to cheer her up, so I decided to show her my dance moves to the music playing in the background. I did some break-dancing moves. Of course, windmill and jackhammer were out of my reach, but I did the moonwalk pretty well and kinda, you know, sort of ...."

"C'mon, Ray! Be out with it," Kamal urged Ray on.

"Well, I did some turn around spins and subsequently attempted a split..."

Adam and Kamal chuckled. "So, were you able to put the Jean-Claude Van Damme split move on her?" Adam asked rhetorically.

"I wish. Man, the only thing that split was my pant," Ray recalled as his friends burst into uncontrollable laughter. Ray was unfaced and continued, but that was not the worst part."

"So, what happened?" Kamal inquired.

"I must have torn some ligaments of some sort or just overstretched them. Boy, I couldn't get up. My thighs hurt so bad and Desiree had to help me up while she was laughing hysterically at my predicament."

Adam and Kamal could not control their laughter.

Ray pointed accusatory fingers at his buddies and remarked, "You guys are just like Desiree. You mean that you do not realize that it wasn't funny."

Unfortunately for Ray, the more he spoke, the funnier it sounded to his friends, and Kamal remarked, "If that had taken place now, it would have a million hits on YouTube or Instagram."

"You are not serious! Anyway, we left the quadrangle immediately after that. Desiree brightened up, laughing at my expense."

"I guess that we can also, you know, agree that you actually achieved your objective at the cost of your pants!" Adam joked.

"Very funny!" Ray responded with tongue in cheek. "The truth is that it is really frustrating that despite all my efforts, past and present, Desiree still treats me badly."

"I feel your pain, but I genuinely hope that things will get better with both of you," Kamal remarked with a ray of hope.

Adam then remarked, "I am so sorry for your plight. I don't know what else to say other than to wish you and your family well and safe delivery."

"I feel for you, but at the same time, I am still thankful for you. Having a child is a blessing from the Almighty. Perhaps, this child will even bring you closer to Desiree rather than away from her, much unlike how you are feeling right now," Kamal reiterated.

"Thanks, guys. I really appreciate your messages of optimism. Let's hope that it works out that way," Ray submitted.

Part Two

Surreal and So Real:
The story of Adam

Part Two: Section One:
The Unexpected Meeting

"I started second-guessing why I agreed to meet Aneida's parents for dinner. They had come to town from Florida for a reunion with their friends. Aneida had mentioned that after her father retired from his job in DC, her parents sold their house and moved to a warmer climate in Florida as many people do."

"You mean...like many rich people do?" Kamal asked rhetorically.

"I don't know how rich or poor her parents are. Well, I guess they are rich enough. Anyway, Aneida has not seen her parents in two years. After her divorce from Phillip the flip flop, she had been in a cycle of taking care of herself, her children, and working, and had not been able to take any meaningful vacation to go anywhere."

Adam continued, "I was conflicted about meeting Aneida's parents. I felt that it might end up encouraging her that there is hope for an Adam-Aneida combination when an Adam-Nora combination is really what is on my radar. I know that Aneida is a good woman and she probably would make a great mother for her kids and mine. Our children would probably get along and be brothers and sisters and keep one another company and grow together, making parenting a little easier for both of us. I mean, the children can play together, go to school together...."

Kamal gave Ray a small jab at the elbow to draw his

attention to the advantages and the rationale why Aneida is a much better choice for Adam which happened to be what he has been telling him all along.

Adam noticed it but chose to ignore it and continued. "On the day that I was supposed to have dinner with Aneida's parents, I suddenly became anxious. I couldn't understand why. It was as if I wanted them to approve of me. I wanted to make a good impression, but I couldn't understand why it suddenly mattered to me when the only reason why I agreed to come was because I just felt pity or something like that for her. Maybe I just wanted to help her feel better, and give the impression that things were looking up for her when she met with her parents or something.

"I had to quickly remind myself of the decorum of meeting in-laws for the first time. It was all about the first impressions. Is it only for young lovers or is it applicable to those in rebound like Aneida and me too? I wondered." Adam then chuckled, saying that Aneida is on offensive rebound and he is on defensive rebound.

"That would mean that you are perfect for each other," Kamal interjected.

Adam simply looked away from him and faced Ray and continued his tale. "Anyway, I later settled for a suit with a shirt and with a tie so that if I get there and the family was casual, I could simply remove my tie and I would fit right in as being business casual.

"Nice move," Ray remarked. "It is better to be over-dressed than to be under-dressed when going for an important meeting."

"Thank you. I am still formidable in the game," Adam complimented himself. "Well, I got there early. In actual fact, about thirty minutes early. The last thing you would want is to be late while meeting a prospective father and mother-in-law. It sends the message that one is irresponsible. The reservation was in Aneida's name. I brought a fruit basket as a gift for her family."

"Why the fruit basket?" Ray asked. "Pardon me. I crossed such a river with Desiree's parents a very long time ago without a refresher course."

"I couldn't think of anything else. I know that fruits do not generally offend people as a gift, and they are not expensive. Do you think I should have brought something else?"

Marrying somebody's daughter is a way of reaping the fruit of somebody else's labor. Just think about it!

"Not really. I was just curious," Ray explained.

"When I mentioned my party to the usher at the reception area of the restaurant, I was directed to a private room in the restaurant. I was surprised. Well, apparently, Aneida also wanted to have a good first impression."

I ordered a glass of ginger ale while I waited at our table for our remaining party. I was watching the television overhead when about ten minutes later, Aneida walked in with her parents. I was shocked to my bone marrow."

"Why? What happened?" Ray asked.

"I know her father very well," Adam replied.

"Wow! It is really a small world," Ray responded.

"Yes. It is a tiny world," Adam concurred.

"How did you know her father?" Kamal inquired.

"You would not believe this. Her father was really her stepfather. He was my assigned academic mentor in medical school and my attending physician in postgraduate training."

"Interesting," Kamal remarked.

"The story was that Dr. Dan Howard married Aneida's mum when she was two years old. Her biological father, Captain Neumann, died in an army helicopter crash during a training mission over a mountain area in Colorado. That was why Aneida has a different last name. Dr. Howard had known Aneida's mum when they were both taking undergraduate courses in college. Well, Dr. Howard and Aneida's mum had two other children together."

"Very interesting," Kamal remarked again. "I think this actually works to your advantage. I do not think that her family will object to your marrying their daughter."

"Are you kidding me? Dr. Howard was very happy to see me. He would love for me to marry his daughter yesterday. Somehow, he did not realize that his daughter was talking about me. We had lost contact a few years ago, and he was not aware that my wife died. The last time I saw him was a few years ago, and I had missed his retirement party."

"So, what time did you guys fix for the wedding?" Kamal asked midway between joking and being very serious.

"That is the problem," Adam responded. "Dr. Howard meant so much to me. He was my academic and career mentor. I actually became a gastroenterologist because of his influence."

"Wow!" Ray exclaimed.

"Yeah! Dr. Howard was one of the most respected professors and clinical faculty in the medical center. He was well-liked and respected by the faculty and staff. He was a professor's professor and retired as an Emeritus Magnificent Professor of Medicine. In fact, one of my most memorable days in the medical school was the first day that I shadowed Dr. Howard in the clinic as my instructor in the Introduction to Physical Diagnosis course. That first day of learning from him was so memorable. He was such a funny doctor who enjoyed what he did. He told us that gastroenterologists are the happiest doctors in the world because they get to smell laughing gas all day long while performing a colonoscopy. You would think that it should be the opposite. He related well with patients explaining his treatment plans, and he has this jovial way of connecting with his patients that makes them very relaxed."

"Interesting!" Kamal remarked.

"He was informed that one of the patients he was to perform a colonoscopy on was very nervous. We were with him when he went to obtain the permit for the procedure, the informed consent, as it is called. He explained the procedure to the patient in very simple and plain language. He then told the patient that part of the procedure involved putting gas into the colon of the patient. He then asked the patient:

"So, if during the procedure, you feel like passing gas, what do you think you should do?"

"I should hold on to it," he replied.

"Wrong answer. To the contrary, I want you to pass the gas and make it loud."

The patient chuckled, thinking he was joking. "Really?" he asked. "That would be so embarrassing!"

Absolutely not! Do you know how to pass gas?" Dr. Howard asked him.

"Er...Er...Y-y-yes," He mumbled to answer.

"Excellent! Otherwise, I would have to ask one of these nurses to give you a quick demonstration of how to pass gas. He then pointed to one of the nurses and remarked that Tracy is one of our gas passing champions. I can tell her to give you a quick tutorial if you want."

The patient started smiling and said, "I am good. No demonstration is necessary."

"So, this is what I want you to do. If you feel like passing gas during this procedure, I want you to make it loud, and when you make it loud, you will make me proud. Okay. Make it loud, make me proud. Got it?"

Make me proud
Pass the gas
Don't hold it
Release the gas
Don't hoard it
Expel the gas
Don't pity it
Make it loud
Make me proud.

The man started laughing. He also asked him if he had any allergies. The man replied that he does not have any allergies.

"You mean no allergies to drugs, cats, mother-in-law, father-in-law?" Dr. Howard asked.

"No allergies to them," He affirmed.

"Do you have allergies to money?" Dr. Howard asked the patient.

"Nope. Well, money may be allergic to me, but I am certainly not allergic to it," he replied, laughing.

"At this point, the patient was having fun waiting for his colonoscopy. The fact is that Dr. Howard related well with people and he was very approachable to medical students and other trainees as well. He loved to teach in a non-threatening manner. As medical students, he always emphasized being well dressed for patient encounters. To him, it means that you should be in a shirt and tie. Then he told us that suprapubic ties are the standard. We did not quite follow and sought clarification. He then told us that a necktie can be 'too short' that it ends up as an epigastric tie, just 'short' to become a paraumbilical tie, or too long to be a pubic tie. Therefore, we should practice well to ensure that our neckties are always suprapubic."

Dr. Howard told us that his roommate in the first year of medical school later founded a tech company after dropping out of medical school. He left medical school out of frustration that things almost always remain the same. He was having a hard time in school and blamed the medical curriculum. He complained that things are not adapting and evolving like technology.

Their medical physiology professor replied to him that human beings are not machines or robots that will have 1.0 and 2.0 series. Human physiology does not change. Our understanding may continue to improve. The facial nerve is not going to suddenly decide to supply the gluteus maximus muscle in order to expand its territory. His roommate insisted that physiology changes, to which the professor replied that 'when physiology changes, we call it pathology.' He told us that his roommate later changed career.

Dr. Howard never missed an opportunity to tease the nurses. He told us there are three categories of nurses.

1. Staph Nurses: They are also known as RN, i.e., Real Nurses or Regular Nurses. Most nurses are in this category. They do their jobs very well, but they also spread their staphylococcus if they did not wash their hands properly. He told us that according to medical historians, Ignaz Semmelweis discovered the cause of puerperal sepsis came from staph nurses who were working in labor and delivery.

2. Bold Staph Nurses: They are also known as BSN. They are resistant Staph nurses and are typically the union leaders. They are usually the ones who negotiate with management regarding pay, benefits and they order union strikes as necessary.

3. Diff Nurses: Most people think it means they are like C diff which rears its ugly head after antibiotics to treat infections with the assumption that Diff Nurses fight union leaders when they agree, and

broker deals with management. Some people believe that Diff nurses are Differentiated Nurses, that is, specialty nurses like endoscopy nurses, Intensive Care Unit (ICU) nurses, and Dialysis nurses, but in reality, it simply means Difficult Nurses.

The nurses were rolling their eyeballs and shaking their heads; that's how we knew he wasn't telling us the complete truth about that classification.

"Anyway, in the end, Dr. Howard told me that he would love to see Aneida and me together," Adam concluded.

"What did you say?" Ray inquired.

"I smiled, but I was tongue-tied," Adam replied. "I felt that I should not have come to dinner. I felt a bit trapped. On my right side is Aneida, on my left side is Dr. Howard, but my heart is with Nora...."

"Who does not want it," Kamal interjected.

Author's note: Should you marry somebody at the recommendation of someone you respect or as a favor to somebody else?

"Eventually, I told Dr. Howard that my relationship with Aneida is a work in progress." Adam continued rambling, "I really did not know what to tell him. He was my career mentor, my scientific mentor..."

"Why should that prevent you from telling him how you feel? If you are truly not interested in this lady, you should not waste her time. You should say *no* so that she can make herself available to others," Ray emphasized decisively.

"Or perhaps, he really wanted to say *yes*, but he is too chicken to say so, because he is still hoping against hope that Nora will somehow fall in love with him," Kamal suggested.

"It is complicated. Honestly, I am not so sure. I really feel that Aneida will be a great mum, but my heart is still with Nora," Adam explained.

After a brief period of awkward silence, Adam continued, "The truth is that I am really confused now, more than ever before. I am not so sure if things will work out with Nora especially with her mum and I am actively trying to get Nora out of my head, but the feeling I have for her in my heart remains unchanged. I still really love her."

"Then, work on convincing her mum that you are going to take good care of her," Ray suggested.

"It is more complicated than that. There are too many moving parts now. I am—"

"I got it. Eureka!" Kamal exclaimed. "I have the perfect solution for you, my friend."

"What is it?" Adam asked Kamal with excitement.

"Become younger!" Kamal replied.

Adam gave Kamal a dirty look and shook his head in disappointment.

Part Two: Section Two:
The Unusual Meeting

Adam related to his friends that he saw Nora get into her car after school dismissal one afternoon. He quickened his steps to catch up with her before she drove away. As he approached the car, he noticed that a lady was sitting in the passenger side of the car. Adam peeped through the driver's side glass and remarked, "Hi Nora, you did not tell me that your younger twin sister came to school to check on you." He then looked at the passenger and introduced himself, "Hi, I am Adam."

"Hi, my name is Norma," Nora's sister sitting on the passenger seat replied.

"I am Normal too, but I can't speak for her," Adam replied jokingly while pointing at Nora. "Nice to finally meet you, Norma."

"Nice to meet you too, Adam," Norma responded and started giggling. She looked at her sister and then at Adam and giggled repeatedly.

Adam continued, "Guys, if an apple doesn't fall far from the tree, then sister apples probably will be falling at the same spot. Norma is a very cute chick too. She has this incredible laughter that will make you laugh without knowing why you are laughing."

"You are not planning to switch over to Norma, are you?" Ray asked Adam while pretending to be serious with the question.

"Of course not! She is my sister-in-law," Adam replied as if the question was a blaspheme.

"Did you mean sister-out-law? You are really crazy. Nora has not married you, and you are calling Norma your sister-in-law. You know that you are going to face a major obstacle with her family, and they may not let you marry their daughter," Kamal voiced his opinion.

Adam did not respond to Kamal's pessimism but continued his tale. "A few weeks later, I met Norma in a grocery store. After exchanging greetings, I asked about Nora."

"She is doing okay," Norma replied.

Adam then lamented, "I am not sure what I did that made Nora hate me so much."

"I am not sure what to tell you, but she doesn't hate you," Norma corrected him.

"Why is she avoiding me then? She doesn't respond to my communications. She ignores me," Adam complained, sounding frustrated.

"Things may not be the way you are perceiving it," Norma opined.

"What do you mean?" Adam sought clarification.

"I don't know what to tell you or whether I should even tell you, but the truth is that she actually l-l-l-likes you." Norma hesitated and stammered.

Adam swallowed his saliva and almost choked on it because of the pleasantly surprising information that he just heard that Nora likes him. His heart got a glimmer of hope.

"Why is she avoiding me then?" Adam inquired.

"It is complicated, and I really can say anything about it. Not my place. Sorry."

"Please Norma, you don't have to tell me the detail. Just give me an idea about what the problem is to put my mind at rest. I send her poems and she doesn't read them. I mean...."

"I wouldn't say that," Norma interjected.

"What do you mean?" Adam inquired again.

"I don't know whether I should tell you or not, but the truth is she reads all your poems. Actually, she reads them over and over again, especially the one in which you expressed that you don't really know why you love her so much. She really thinks that you are a good writer," Norma replied and then covered her mouth as if she had just revealed a top-secret.

Adam downplayed his enormous happiness and just smiled. His heart busted into love flames like the Olympic torch, and he developed goosebumps.

"C'mon Norma, your secret is safe with me. So, why is she trying to make me believe that she hates me?" Adam pressed further.

"To the contrary...well, I am not saying she likes you, but if she likes you, I mean, things may still not work out...from circumstances she cannot control," Norma struggled to explain without explaining.

"Why? We can always work it out," Adam tried to reassure Norma.

Almost immediately, Norma's phone rang with a melodious tune. She looked at her phone and gestured to Adam to please not say anything. Then, she answered the phone and after a few seconds, replied, "Yes, mum," and hung up.

She then faced Adam and remarked, "I am so sorry, but I need to go. Mum is in the parking lot waiting for me." She turned and hurriedly quickened her pace towards the checkout lane.

Adam was unsure whether to continue the conversation and follow her or to just respect her apparently implied 'please don't follow me.' In the end, he did not follow her, but rather, he ruminated over their conversation. Adam started wondering if Nora's mum was really the major barrier, and if so, why was she so adversarial when she doesn't know him in person. *Why? Why?* He asked himself without any answer. He thought again of following Norma and asking her why her mum is in opposition, but he advised himself against such a move. He decided to let her go for now. He was convinced that he will be able to continue to get information from her as an insider later. It made sense not to drive her away. Yes, that made more sense, and he could call her later. As he watched her exit the front door of the store, the fallacy of this plan struck him like a lightning bolt—he did not know her phone number!

For a few weeks afterward, Nora seemed withdrawn, but would not talk to Adam about what was bothering her. However, one Friday afternoon after dismissal, Nora told Adam that her father would like to meet him the following day at six p.m. if he was available. Adam quickly replied that he was available even though he knew that he was on call at the hospital. She did not expand why the father wanted him to come, but given the information from Norma earlier, maybe they just wanted to meet him.

Nora's father is 11 years older than Nora's mum. They married when she was 19 years old. Nora's mum was an only child, and her parents wanted her to marry early. Nora's father apparently noticed that his daughter has not been cheerful and has not been eating well. It was obvious that something was bothering her. He called her and talked to her. She broke down crying because she felt emotionally overwhelmed by her circumstances. Her father comforted her and talked to her mum. They argued. Nora's mum raised the issue of the wide age gap of 22 years between Nora and Adam.

Nora's father replied, "Well, that is just twice our own age differences, but it is not a big deal. Can't you see that Nora may actually like this guy?"

"She shouldn't," her mum replied.

"Why?" her father queried.

"He is too old for her. She should get somebody who is only two or three years older than her. That way, they can be friends."

"But I am 11 years older than you, and we have a good marriage. Did you regret marrying me?"

"Absolutely not. However, we got married in the olden days. Things are different now."

"Says who?"

"All I am saying is that things have changed from our youth days. In the modern era, ladies tend to marry their age mates rather than somebody much older."

"Does that mean that they are more happily married? Does that mean that they have more fulfilling marriages than their parents?" He asked his wife without waiting for an answer.

"Well, the couple tends to be closer when there isn't too much difference in their ages."

"That may be just your assumption. Why do they end up with more divorces?"

Nora's mum had no answer.

In the end, they reached a compromise to invite Adam to dinner and get to know him. If he is not a good candidate, that will make it obvious to Nora too, and it will be easier for her to move on. Nora's dad opined that Nora has a soft spot for Adam.

Adam continued. "On M day, I woke up early. Actually, I couldn't sleep well overnight."

"What is M day?" Kamal asked him.

"The Meeting Day," Adam explained. "The day I will finally have the opportunity to present myself and show Nora's family that I am Nora's soulmate."

Kamal chuckled.

Adam ignored him and continued. "I quickly went to the hospital to make my rounds. I already made up my mind about what I would wear to dinner. It was going to be my favorite black suit. I planned to look so official, even penguins all over the world will be jealous. So, I went from the hospital to the ABC Megastore to look for a gift for Nora's family. When I got to the door, the young employee at the entrance, whose task was to check membership cards and count the people coming into the store, suddenly shouted very loudly in excitement."

"Why?" Ray asked.

"I was surprised too and wondered what was going on until the guy came closer to me and remarked, 'Dude! You are still wearing a pager! Wow!'"

"I guess he realized that you must be really old," Kamal responded in jest.

"That was not the worst part," Adam continued. He then called another guy from the electronic department close to the entrance, saying, "Sam, Sam come and see this."

Ray and Kamal started laughing.

"When Sam came over, he said to him. 'Wow! This guy is still using a pager.' Sam looked at my waist and low and behold. I had my black Metrocell wireless pager firmly attached. At that point, I did not know whether to feel embarrassed or not, but I was in such a great mood because I was going to meet Nora's family, I just decided to play along."

"Does it work?" Sam asked me.

"Yeah. It works. Would you like to hear it?" I responded.

"Yes," they responded in unison.

"I took out my smartphone and paged myself, and the pager came alive with the traditional annoying beeping sound that all medical interns hate with passion from the beginning of time. These guys were elated. Somehow, it didn't occur to them that I may be a physician. They were too fixated on the pager. Interestingly, it didn't strike them that I paged myself using a smartphone. The way they behaved would make you think that I just time traveled from the nineteenth century."

"Anyway, I went inside the store, and I got a big gift basket with many assorted goodies, different kinds of chocolate and truffles, fragrances, home decorations, et cetera. When I got to the checkout lane, my pager truly went off, making the people around me startled. I am sure most of them have never heard a pager go off before. The closest they probably heard to it would be the alarm clock. It was a disaster in the making."

"What happened?" Ray inquired.

"The page was from the emergency department of the hospital. They are requesting an emergency consultation for a foreign body ingestion. The time was almost two-thirty in the afternoon. I had less than four hours until my dinner meeting with my in-laws. My head exploded. Why me? Why today? Why this time? I became really angry. Unfortunately, things only got worse at the checkout lane."

"Why?" Ray asked Adam.

"I guess it was my not-so-lucky day. The specific item I

picked for my father-in-law, a comfy pair of bedroom slippers for him to wear with his bathrobe, did not ring up at the checkout lane. They used the radar price gun, but it still did not work, and they wouldn't take my word for its price. So, the attendant put on her flashing light for price check by the supervisor. Ordinarily, I would have just told them to take off the item, but on this day, it was the only personalized gift for my main supporter in their household. I could not afford to leave it behind. After a time-consuming price check which felt like an eternity, I finally left the store utterly distraught. I was very apprehensive about what would happen at the hospital and how it would delay me further. Unfortunately, the consultation was a case of love affair gone awry."

"What happened?" Kamal inquired.

"Mr. Charlie de Lavabeaux, a French gentleman who just completed his doctorate in Civil Engineering from the University of Greenbelt, wanted to propose marriage to his girlfriend in style. He really could have just got on one knee like normal people would or even on both knees, I wouldn't care. Unfortunately, this love-drunk guy decided that he needed to do something very memorable for his girlfriend on the most important day in recent memory for me," Adam was getting angry while reliving this moment again.

"Relax Adam," Ray tried to calm him down.

Adam sighed and continued. "As I was saying earlier, this loverboy had a romantic grand plan of proposing to his girlfriend during a romantic lunch date, but he wanted to pass an engagement ring into her mouth during a passionate French kiss instead of just going down on one knee like a normal guy. Unfortunately, he started getting anxious regarding his proposal. He started considering the fact that she may actually reject his proposal. However, he decided to still go through with it. He decided to go ahead with his plan after they were given their drinks while waiting for the food they ordered. He put the ring in his mouth in anticipation of a memorable French kiss...."

"But why French kiss?" Ray interrupted Adam.

"I guess it is supposed to be superior to an English kiss or an American kiss. After all, the French are the most romantic men in the world, according to polls in France by the French people." Adam responded. He then continued, "Loverboy then lovingly pulled his girlfriend towards him, but he felt the urge to clear his throat and he coughed. While trying desperately not to choke, he inadvertently swallowed the ring."

"Poor guy!" Kamal remarked.

"Poor me!" Adam retorted. "He was lucky that the ring did not go into his trachea. I was unlucky that the ring did not go into his trachea because if it had gone into his trachea, he would have been a patient for the Ear Nose and Throat (ENT) surgeons or the pulmonary team on call and not me."

"C'mon, Adam!" Ray remarked.

"I know," Adam threw his hands up in the air. "Well, I actually pity the guy in the end. I really felt sorry for him."

"What happened?" Kamal inquired.

"He informed his girlfriend of what just happened. She did not believe him at first, but then he showed her the ring case. It was a stunning navy-blue velvet top case with gold sides that opens in a clasping move that is both graceful and silent, with an interior that is soft, well-cushioned and screaming of exquisite luxury beauty. Apparently, she asked him for the case. On touching it and feeling all the love the case had to offer, she could only imagine what the ring would look like. She got up from her seat and in a true emergency, they rushed to the door. She asked loudly where the nearest hospital was letting the waiters and the people in the restaurant realize that she needed to get him to the emergency department right away. He quickly left some money on the table as they hurried through the door. He was still coughing and was distraught at the loss of the ring."

Adam took a sip of his drink and continued the unfortunate tale. "In the emergency department, the plain abdominal X-ray showed the ring is in the stomach. The news of what happened to Loverboy spread like wildfire in harmattan among the nurses in the main medical emergency care area, the pediatric emergency care area, the surgical emergency care area and the fast track areas of the emergency department. The nurses were full of pity for him on hearing the turn of events of this love story. "How romantic?" the charge nurse remarked to me when I got to the emergency department. I had initially recommended watchful waiting since it was an 18 karat rose gold engagement ring with French cut halo diamond, which means that the ring is not made of easily corrosive materials. The patient was breathing on his own without any problems; he did not have any symptoms of obstruction and was swallowing his saliva easily. Furthermore, the small ring can easily pass from the stomach into the small bowel, make it through the large bowel and he can pass it in his feces in a couple of days. It sounded like a scandal to the nurses when I told them of this. Some of them remarked with one indescribable word, 'Ewww' at my suggestion of watchful waiting and stool recovery strategy. The Loverboy started crying which drew a lot of pity from the nurses in the emergency department. The look on the faces of all the ladies in the emergency department that day—from the transportation orderly, sanitation specialist, nurse aides, and nursing staff—was a universal screaming that when put in words would be 'Seriously? You want to kill this fantastic love story and let this love ring come out from the other end?' I explained the risk of the procedure and encouraged him to ignore the ladies' comments, but he did not want to take the chance of the ring coming out with the brown stuff. Not only because he will have to be collecting, examining and straining his poop, but he was also fearful that the ring might get stuck somewhere in his intestine, and he may then need major surgery to remove it. I explained to him that given the size of the ring, his lack of any significant medical or surgical history that relates to the abdomen and intestines, it is highly unlikely that it will get stuck."

"Although watchful waiting will save me some time to go and take care of my own love story with Nora, the altruism in me kicked in, and I spoke with the anesthesiologist. We decided to help the guy out and remove the ring endoscopically before it leaves the stomach because if it leaves the stomach, there is nothing more we can do for him. He will have to wait for it to emerge from the other end.

Fortunately, there was no other emergency surgery ongoing or being planned at that time. Therefore, shortly before five p.m., we removed the ring. Typically, foreign bodies removed at endoscopic procedures or surgery are sent to pathology, but we made an exception in this case. 'There was no need to send this prized love item to pathology in formalin,' we had joked in a lighter mood after successfully removing the love ring. I left the hospital immediately after the procedure to go home and change in order to save my own love affair, only to be called from the hospital by the recovery room nurse that Loverboy did not have a ride home."

"What did you mean that he had no ride?" I queried. "His girlfriend can take him home."

Then, there was an awkward silence. Then, she mumbled, "em...em...she left as soon as you told her that the procedure was successful and you had removed the ring."

"What? She couldn't even wait for him to be discharged?" I couldn't believe it. The fact was that he had left his car at the restaurant where he rendezvous with his girlfriend in the botched engagement proposal. Now that he had just awoken from sedation, he is not supposed to drive or operate heavy machinery for 24 hours.

The nurse told me on the phone that she said that she had to leave because she has an appointment with her hairdresser and did not want to miss it. They found this out after they called her to let her know his status and she told them over the phone that she is not coming back to the hospital as she does not want to miss her hair braiding appointment.

"That is so bad!" Ray exclaimed.

"To me, the most shocking part was that many of the ladies who were encouraging me to remove the ring endoscopically and wanted the poor loverboy to undergo endoscopy to remove the ring later told me that they understood why the lady made such a selfish and bizarre decision to leave her loverboy in the hospital. They gave a lot of unbelievable excuses such as, "She may be charged a no-show surcharge," "She may lose her deposit," "She may lose her spot," "Her thin braids are likely to be an eight-hour marathon hairdressing experience so the earlier she gets there, the better."

"He is lucky that she is not the one who swallowed the ring during the kiss," Kamal opined.

"That is his silver lining right there," Ray concurred. "Moreover, he can give the ring to another lucky girl, so long as he doesn't tell her where the ring had been. It was unbelievable that she left him in the hospital to keep her hairdo appointment. How unappreciative women can be! This guy just risked his life for her, to impress her and she left him here just for a hairdo? I guess we can never understand women. They are too self-centered, parochial, and unappreciative. I mean this is a guy who is trying to do something truly special. Unfortunately, it did not work out that way. He even risked his life, getting it out rather than watchful waiting. He wanted to give her a lovely engagement ring from his heart and stomach rather than his heart and his rear. Yet, he was left behind by the same babe to wallow in his misery."

Ray took a sip of his drink and continued his ranting on behalf of loverboy. "What's up with ladies and their hairdos anyway?"

"What did you mean? The hair is a major part of the beauty of a woman, and every woman wants to be beautiful," Adam countered.

"That is not what I meant. See, a woman spends a lot of time and money on her hair. Simple stuff with styling takes a few hours, but braiding takes a whole week. They tell you that they did it for you, but they don't let you touch the hair in appreciation of its beauty," Ray lamented.

"Maybe, it is painful for them. They just don't confess to guys to let us know that they are suffering trying to impress us," Kamal suggested.

"Is that why they are always hitting their heads after such a marathon hair work-out?" Adam queried.

"Nope. That patting of their heads is when their hair is itching them," Ray answered.

"Really? How did you know that?" Adam asked Ray, being surprised.

"I saw Desiree doing it before, and I accused her that she will deliberately hit herself on the head so that when I call her to come and do her comfort duties, she will give me her bogus excuse that she has a headache. She was furious that day and told me that she was not trying to give herself a stroke or an aneurysm as I claimed but that she has an itching discomfort in her hair."

"Interesting!" Adam exclaimed. "Why don't they just scratch their heads like we do?"

"Well, I guess that is what being a lady is all about," Ray explained.

"You mean suffering, pretending, and smiling?" Adam commented.

"All I know is that it is a lady thing. Women will do stuff that will inconvenience them to get the attention of men, and after they have our attention, then they enjoy rebuffing us. It absolutely makes no sense."

"I am not following your argument," Adam expressed.

"Let me give you an easy example. Ladies wear pumps or high heel shoes, not because they like the pain it gives them in their feet, ankles, or knees, but because they know that it makes them elegant and increases their confidence in the way they look. They appear taller and are able to shake their bodies in a way that makes us go gaga. Unfortunately, when their husbands are now in the gaga mood, they tell them to go-go and leave them alone. This is very unfair," Ray concluded.

Adam shook his head and remarked, "Why do guys always want to go overboard when they are smitten with love? Is it really the grandeur of the proposal that will make a lady say yes or no?" Adam asked without waiting for an answer and continued his ranting, "C'mon, no need to go overboard with a proposal. Guys will be jumping out of a plane, sky diving or bungee jumping just to ask a simple question. I tell you if I were a lady, and a guy jumped out of the plane just to ask if I would marry him, I am going to say *no*."

"Why?" Ray asked Adam being quite surprised.

"Because I will be afraid, wondering what he will then do

to impress me if I say *yes*. Is he going to jump again, this time without a parachute?"

"C'mon Adam. Guys are not that stupid. They may want to impress a chick, but not commit suicide." Ray disagreed.

"For me, I kept it really simple. 'Nora, I have feelings for you. I love you, and I want to spend the rest of my life with you.' Really simple."

Time well spent
I want to love you
Every second of the minute
I want to be in your arms
Every minute of the hour
I want to be holding your hands
Every hour of the day
I want to be in your presence
Every week of the month
I want to be with you
Every month of the year
I want to sit with you
Every year of the decade
I want to stand with you
Every decade of the century
I want to love you
For my entire lifetime
I want you in my life
Forever and ever
I love you.

"Since you are so old…almost as old as dirt, did she ask you how many minutes that would be?" Kamal asked Adam sarcastically.

"C'mon! Don't remain a fool forever." Adam responded while pretending to be concerned about Kamal's level of understanding. "Dying and living has nothing to do with age at the individual level. Collectively, people will tend to die around certain ages of life expectancy. However, individually, you will check out when your time comes, whether young or old."

"So, what happened to loverboy?" Ray asked.

"The nurses were able to call one of his friends to pick him up," Adam responded.

"Poor guy!" Ray pitied loverboy again.

"By the time I got home and got ready for my big date with Nora's family it was already 5:45 p.m.. There was no way I could make it to their home before six p.m. I felt embarrassed, but I knew that it made more sense to inform them that I was going to be a few minutes late because of work-related issues. I sent a text message to Nora that I had an emergency procedure to do in the hospital earlier, but I was on my way. You guys will not believe this."

"What?" Ray and Kamal asked in unison.

"That day was really a D-Day!"

"D-Day as in, you invaded Nora's home?" Kamal asked in jest.

"Silly! No, D-Day as in Disaster Day," Adam explained. "It was as if nothing went right that day."

"Disturbingly interesting!" Kamal opined. "What happened?"

"I was already going to be late to a dinner with my in-laws, as soon as I got to the main highway, there was an unusual traffic jam. Apparently, there was an accident after I passed by the place about half an hour earlier. We later heard that a guy was texting while riding his bike on the wrong side of the road."

"Texting while riding a bicycle?" Ray questioned. "What is smart technology doing to people these days?"

"Apparently, making us more stupid!" Adam responded. "So, this guy was texting on his bike. He then hit a pothole and was thrown off his bike into an oncoming vehicle. The driver of the vehicle tried to avoid him much as he could but still ended up hitting him. According to the local news later, he sustained major, but non-life-threatening injuries. The ambulance left soon after I got to the area of the accident. The problem was that the ambulance was blowing its siren but was cruising at 50 miles per hour on Beltway I-95 when the speed limit is 65 miles per hour. We could not figure out if the driver of the ambulance was new at this job or just got his driver's license. The other motorists were confused on the beltway. We were wondering whether we should keep going on the other lanes and essentially overtaking an ambulance that was blowing its siren or were we not supposed to do that. So, the scene on the beltway was a relatively slow-moving ambulance in front and lots of vehicles following it. Fortunately, the ambulance only went three miles on the beltway before it exited onto local lanes towards the nearest trauma center."

Adam took a sip of his drink and continued. "By the time I got to the main feeder road close to Nora's home address, it was already 6:35 pm. I ran into another traffic jam. I called Nora to explain my predicament, but she did not pick up. So, I left a voice message. I was already panicking that I did not even notice that she did not reply my original text message informing her of my delay due to the loverboy's love problems."

Suddenly, Adam paused and looked at his friends with a genuinely concerned look. "Guys, if you have a true emergency and you need to call to talk to someone right away, do not call a woman!" He advised.

"Why?" Kamal asked. "Is it because she will be too emotional and may panic?"

"No, it is because her phone will be in her handbag in silent mode or the vibration mode and the vibration will be muffled by whatever things she keeps in those expensive for nothing handbags! How many times have you ever called a woman and she picked up your call right away?" Adam asked, rhetorically.

"You have a point there," Ray agreed.

"After a short drive, I realized that the slowdown in the side street was because a cop pulled somebody over on the road at an exit, thereby blocking everybody trying to make a right turn. The cop did not tell the motorist to go to an area with a shoulder or a parking lot to complete his charges. That is so stupid. It caused unnecessary traffic stoppage. Suddenly, this cop put on his emergency light and siren and swerved dangerously to catch another motorist with a broken taillight. It was as if he was in a ticket-writing frenzy. What do they teach these cops in the police academy these days? The time was then 6:50 p.m. When I eventually got to where the cop was busy writing the ticket, I felt like winding down my passenger side window and yelling to the cop, 'Give yourself a ticket too!'"

"If you had done that, you probably would have never made it to the dinner at all," Ray responded.

"I was very frustrated and angry. Eventually, I rang the doorbell at the front entrance of Nora's family home at precisely 7:03 pm. Nora's dad opened the door promptly. I introduced myself immediately. He shook my hand and welcomed me into the living room."

"We have been waiting and worried about you," Nora's dad remarked as he beckoned me to sit on the sofa.
"I am so sorry, sir, but I had to do an emergency procedure in the hospital, and the traffic was not friendly to me today," Adam struggled to explain. "I sent a text message to Nora and also called her, but there was no pick-up, so I left her a message to let her know, sir."

Apparently, Nora was dealing with her own issues with her mother too. She had left her phone on vibration mode upstairs in her bedroom and did not see any of Adam's messages.

"I presented the gift I brought as Nora's dad announced my presence so that the rest of the family can come to welcome me. I became a little apprehensive, and then I got the greatest shocker of my adult life."
"What happened?" Kamal asked.
"It was Nora's mother, Zinnia the plant. That was what we called her back then," Adam responded with a sigh.

"You knew her?" Kamal asked in utmost surprise.
"Unfortunately, yes. Just my luck. Of all the women in the world, the woman who hates me the most happened to be the mother of the lady I love the most."
"O my goodness!" Ray remarked.

"Nora's mum and I were mates from elementary school, and we attended the same middle school in Virginia before my family relocated to Maryland, and I attended high school with you, knuckleheads."

"Were you guys dating or something?" Ray asked, being impatient.

"Absolutely not. We were too adversarial to even have any meaningful friendship as kids. Zinnia was this feisty little girl. She was very assertive, confident, and brilliant. We competed for everything. Even though she was this tiny, cute girl, she would not back down for anybody. She was so opinionated, and we argued and disagreed all the time. We had too many of those. There was a time we got our science teacher so angry during science class, that we made the quiet teacher curse biologically."

"What did you mean?" Ray asked.

"During science class one day, we were paired together to do some sort of experiment, but she had too much ego to listen to me. We kept disagreeing with each other, and we ended up spilling the materials that we were supposed to be using. The teacher was so angry with us. He looked at us, and you know that he wanted to use the F-word so badly while addressing us. So, he yelled at us and used a biologic F-word on us instead by saying "What the Flora is wrong with you?" to Zinnia and, "What the Fauna is wrong with you?" to me. Needless to say, he gave us an F grade for the science experiment."

"Well-deserved F grades for both of you," Kamal remarked. "But I am sure that you probably initiated the problem."

"Not at all. You need to know Zinnia in those days. I don't think she has changed much. She only got older." Adam lamented.

"So, you guys never mend fences until you graduated from middle school?" Ray inquired.

"Unfortunately, we never did. In fact, she got her nickname of Zinnia the plant from me in a public forum."

"Wow," Ray exclaimed.

"We were in the conference hall waiting for an event or something which I don't remember anymore. I sat on an empty seat only for Zinnia to walk up to me and claim that she was sitting there before but had momentarily gotten up to put something in her school bag. In my defense, she did not leave anything there to show that she was there previously. Unfortunately, the guys were watching me trying to see if I was going to be 'chicken' and give her the seat and the gals were watching to see what would happen too. In hindsight now, I should have just been the gentleman that I am and just let her have the seat. Unfortunately, back then, I did not know better. So, I refused to get up for her. Since she was also a defiant girl, she did not back off. Rather, she kept insisting that it was her seat. Then, she decided to sit on the armrest of the chair. She gave me a dirty look and remarked, 'You are an animal!' I looked at her too and responded with 'You are a plant.' Our exchange made our classmates burst into uncontrollable laughter. From that day onward in middle school, our classmates called her 'Zinnia the plant' and they called me 'Adam the animal.' Now you see why I am so distraught to think that of all the women in the world, Nora chose to be born by the woman who hates me the most in the world," Adam lamented again.

"Point of correction," Kamal responded. "Nora did not choose her mother."

"I don't care. Why couldn't it be anybody else but Zinnia to be her mother?" Adam continued his lamentation.

"I am beginning to think that you probably like Zinnia and her resemblance is what you saw in Nora that made you become smitten by her love," Kamal opined.

Adam waved his hands and remarked, "Maybe or maybe not. However, having seen them together now, I could see the resemblance too. But why Zinnia? There are over a billion women in the world, why Zinnia? Why? Why?"

"What about her father?" Ray asked.

"Nora's father is a complete gentleman, very liberal. He was the one who made the dinner happen in the first place. The truth is that no guy is ever good enough for the daughter's father." Adam replied.

Ray and Kamal nodded in agreement.

"As far as most fathers are concerned, nobody is ever going to be good enough for their daughters. The typical father is just biting his lower lip and saying 'My sweet pea, if you like this sleazy, fast, smooth-talking, cheeseball guy, it is okay with me as long as you are happy'...he will just keep the sleazy, fast, smooth-talking, cheeseball part to himself. The average father tries not to fail every guy, but rather looks at the bigger picture in the proposed relationship. No father wants to break his daughter's heart. Fathers want to be protective but not over-protective. The problem is that human beings have no knowledge of the unseen and the future. So, nobody truly knows what marriage will be a resounding success and which one will be a colossal failure. Mothers on the other hand sometimes want to fix their perceived personal failures in their own marriages with the marriage of their children. Some of the behaviors they exhibit may be subconscious. Unfortunately, sometimes they let minor issues lead them to miss the bigger picture because they focused on a single issue. Inadvertently, they may make great guys leave their daughters because of trifles," Adam opined.

Adam continued his tale of woes. "Seeing Zinnia increased my anxiety and almost pushed me into despondency. I wasn't too sure what to do anymore. I got up from my seat."

"Zinnia? You are Nora's mum?" Adam asked as if he needed confirmation.

"Adam? You are the Adam Nora was talking about?" Zinnia replied. She also couldn't believe it herself. She then gave a sarcastic laugh.

Nora's dad looked at us and remarked. "You two knew each other?"

"I nodded in affirmation and replied that we were classmates in elementary and middle schools."

"This is interesting," Nora's father remarked as we sat back on the sofa.

"This is crazy interesting," Ray remarked. "So, you are an animal who wants to take a beautiful flower from an angry plant. Good luck with that."

The dinner itself was uneventful. Really uneventful. Nobody spoke for a while. The reality that Adam knew Nora's mum and that their relationship was not the friendly type sucked the enthusiasm out of the dinner. Adam was not sure where to sit at the dining table. He did not know whether this was a traditional family setting where the father sits at the head of the table, the mother on the opposite pole, and the rest sit according to their ages, or if it was free for all as desired. So, he hesitated to come to the table, waiting to let everybody get there first. Adam regretted not reading up some things about table setting and table manners before coming to the dinner. Little did he realize that everything looked formal and official like it was that evening because he was there. Ordinarily, they would sit and eat any way they felt. They were a very cohesive family, and Zinnia runs a tight ship, but nothing was formal. They had just one rule— nobody brings his or her cell phone to the dining table. So, as it was awkward for Adam, it was awkward for his hosts too. Adam just did not know it.

The only thing that kept Adam mentally afloat was his unshaken love for Nora. Seeing her made his problems disappear, and it gave him a glimmer of hope, despite the fact that his nemesis was Nora's mum. Nora's father realized that Adam was not eating. He started watching him and noted that Adam was just too busy looking at Nora throughout.

Thinking of you
I am thinking of you
I am usually thinking of you
I am often thinking of you
I am always thinking of you
I am persistently thinking of you
I am constantly thinking of you
I am forever thinking of you
I will never stop thinking about you
Because I love you

"So, Adam, how do you like the food?" Nora's dad asked Adam when it was too obvious that he had not tasted the food.

Adam was just holding the fork with nothing on his plate.

Adam smiled. He got the message. So, he put the fork down. He took a dinner roll from the breadbasket and placed it on his plate. He took a moderate-sized serving spoonful of hummus on to his plate. He cut off a piece of the bread in his left hand and took the knife. Unfortunately, he could not resist looking at Nora. So, while trying to spread the hummus on the bread he lost focus as he was looking at Nora again and instead, he smeared the hummus on the back of his thumb rather than on the bread he was holding. He immediately realized what has happened and tried not to let anybody know. However, Zinnia, who was sitting next to him, was watching him the whole time as he barely broke his gaze with her daughter. So, she remarked midway between fuming and being ridiculous "I see, that your gaze is still somewhere else."

Adam simply smiled without saying a word. In his mind, he was saying… my lovely Nora

I couldn't help myself
I couldn't help thinking about you
I couldn't help dreaming of you
I couldn't help longing to see you
I couldn't help glancing at you
I couldn't help focusing on you
I couldn't help staring at you
I couldn't help trying to talk to you
I couldn't help striving to work with you
I couldn't help wanting to be with you
I couldn't help hoping to marry you because
I couldn't help being in love with you

Please help me by marrying me
Yes, it is that simple.
I miss you so much
I love you so much

"The food looks great, smelled wonderful, and the little I ate was delicious. My appetite was just for Nora rather than the food," Adam recalled.

"Do you recall what was served?" Kamal asked Adam.

"Hmm! Let's see. There were many delicious treats befitting for welcoming a special person, a son-in-law that I am."

Kamal simply shook his head.

"Initially, they brought some yogurt with some assorted cookies while I was sitting on the sofa. The dinner table had different dishes. There was braised lamb shanks, baked chicken with stuffed mushrooms, and fish. I am not sure the name of the fish, but I tasted it, and it was incredible. There was white rice, shrimp fried rice, and spaghetti. There were mixed vegetables and spinach in a sort of white sauce that I had not seen before. In addition to the potato dinner rolls and hummus, there was also crusty crunchy crispy French baguette with a symphony of crackles reminiscent of a well-coordinated orchestra. There was also extra virgin olive oil."

"Why do they call it that?" Ray asked.

"Call what?" Adam answered a question with a question.

"I mean...why do they refer to olive oil as virgin?" Ray clarified his question.

"I don't know. I guess that it is because nobody had eaten it before," Adam replied.

"Thank God for that, you ignoramus," Kamal chimed in. "Can you really imagine being brought some olive oil after somebody had eaten it? C'mon, man! It has to do the processing and purity of the olive oil."

"Why the extra virgin, then?" Ray inquired again eager to know more.

Before Kamal could respond, Adam chimed in sarcastically, "Extra virgin is more virgin, maybe nobody had smelled it too."

Kamal replied Adam, "You are just crazy. It has to do with the processing too. I think the extra virgin takes a lot longer time to produce. That said, I believe the extra is just telling you that they want more money for the same thing so that you can feel good that you paid more money for something extra."

"So, extra special virgin olive oil will even be better then," Adam remarked chuckling.

"I think you need a shrink," Kamal replied to him.

Adam ignored Kamal and continued his narration. "The dinner was strange. Only the two younger brothers of Nora ate anything substantial. Nora herself was feeling shy where she was sitting. She barely ate. It was as if she wanted a single strand of spaghetti each time, and it seemed somehow to just glide away from her fork. It was the most awkward dinner that almost everybody at the table had ever witnessed. Nora's father ate a bit but kept wondering what was going on with everybody else. Zinnia was just fuming where she was sitting. It was as if she busied herself with keeping an eye on me and watching me like a hawk because I did not break my gaze from Nora. Nora was too shy to look up. She just wished the dinner would be over very soon. Norma ate a bit but could not help feeling the pain that her sister was going through.

The truth is that it was ironic that I totally felt out of place while trying to belong. However, the joy of just being invited to be a guest with this wonderful family and the opportunity to see Nora was enough to make me lose my appetite out of pure, undiluted joy from being in pristine love."

Kamal cleared his throat in jest.

"After the dessert of cheesecake, Turkish delight and pistachio, which I actually ate and enjoyed, we had a brief conversation on tangential topics. I did not know how to start apologizing to Zinnia in order to convince her that 'Whatever happened in middle school stays in middle school' and promise her that I will be the best son-in-law to her. Eventually, I thanked them for the invitation and told them that it was truly an honor to meet them. Just before I stepped out of the front door, Zinnia asked me a perplexing question in the form of a whisper. Unfortunately, I could not muster an immediate answer. So, I pretended as if I did not hear her."

"What was it?" Ray inquired.

"Why are you feverishly fighting furiously for a forbidden fantasy?"

"What a question!" Ray opined.

"I later realized that Nora had been having a smoldering disagreement with her mum for a while, and it increased prior to my arrival in their home. Nora had always been her mummy's pet, but her mum preferred her to be with her friend's son who is just a few months older than her. I got a hint about it from Norma later. Unfortunately, I had complained that Nora did not check her phone or pick it up when I was calling her on my way to their home. I did not realize that she had a much bigger fish to fry. I felt bad for Nora because I made her angry too. I really love her."

<u>Catalog of errors</u>

I got lost
While looking for you
I made you angry
While trying to please you
I caused you to withdraw
While longing for you
I got you arguing with your mum
While expressing my love for you
I pushed you away
While trying to win your heart

I am terribly sorry
For making you worry
It was all because of my passion
I had no malicious intention

I am very sorry
For whatever I have done
That upset you

I do apologize
For whatever I did not do
That annoyed you.

Please forgive me.

I love you

"I did not get a chance to talk to Nora that evening apart from when I mentioned to her regarding the messages that I had sent her concerning the circumstances related to my lateness. When I was leaving Nora's home that evening, I felt as if I was asleep and was watching myself in a nightmare that was just unfolding. I still could not believe that Zinnia is the mother of the lady I love most in this world. The question she asked me bothered me. I felt my world was collapsing. I became paranoid. I looked at Zinnia's vehicle in the driveway as I was going to my car and I could see that it hates me too."

"How so?" Ray inquired.

"It's Virginia tag number was SUX I8U2," Adam recalled.

"Are you sure that you actually saw SUX I8U2? Or were you just dazed from unfulfilled dreams which turned into a nightmare?" Ray doubted Adam's recollection.

"Nope. I am pretty sure it was SUX I8U2," Adam reaffirmed.

"I seriously doubt it. I think you were just hallucinating in delirious confusion over love withdrawal. You probably saw SUX 1842, but your confusing disappointed state made you read eighteen forty-two as I eight U 2, as in 'I hate you too,' as if the license plate of the car was talking to you. Did the squirrel on the tree in front of their house call you nuts too? C'mon! Snap out of it," Ray responded.

Adam sighed and sunk his head into his hands. "The only thing memorable about my going to that dinner was the speeding ticket I got in the mail with the picture of my car asking me to pay them a $40 fine for going at 44 miles per hour in a 30 miles per hour speed trap zone close to Nora's home. Unfortunately, things got much worse about a month later."

Part Two: Section Three: Meeting The Expectation

"**A**fter the school went on break, I was not able to get in touch with Nora. My calls were not answered, and I did not get a callback. She did not respond to my text messages also. Then one afternoon, I went to one of my least favorite places on earth, the Department of Motor Vehicles (DMV), to turn in my tags. Guess who I bumped into?"

"Pegasus? Unicorn?" Kamal responded sarcastically.

"There she was, as radiant as ever. My heart melted like a candle. I could not resist going to talk to her. She was surprised to see me. However, unlike me, she was not so excited to see me. As soon as I greeted her, I started apologizing for what happened at the dinner in their house. That was when I realized that she was actually in DMV with someone."

"What? So fast?" Ray was astonished.

"Well, this young guy stretched out his hand to shake me and introduced himself. 'Hi, I am rich and young,' he said as we shook hands."

"Wait a minute! He actually said, 'I am rich and young' to you?" Ray sought clarification.

"His name is Richard Young, but the way he said it gave the impression that he was saying 'I am rich and young.' Maybe, that is how the brat likes to introduce himself. I later learned that he is the only child of a Wall Street fat cow. His introduction of himself was not the worse part of what this braggart did."

"What did he do?" Kamal asked.

"The stupid spoiled brat looked at Nora and remarked, 'This must be the old dude your mum mentioned' while pointing at me." Adam related with his face turning red in anger.

Kamal tried his best to contain his chuckle by swallowing his saliva. He knew that this sounded really bad for Adam.

"Imagine that nitwit calling me an old dude!" Adam exclaimed. "This was why I was so sure that when he said that 'I am rich and young,' he was actually doing a comparison with me, trying to put me down as if to say that I am old and poor. What has he accomplished by himself in his spoiled rotten life anyway?" Adam snarled.

Maturity

My hair may be slightly gray
But my agility is here to stay
I am definitely not as old
As you might have been told
Calling me old is something I detest
I am younger than my beard may suggest

The fact that I am older than you
Does not make me too old for you
The fact that you are younger than me
Does not make you too young for me
Would you rather a brat who disrespects you
Or a mature one who loves and cares about you?

Ray could feel the disturbance and misdirected anger in Adam's voice. So, he interjected.

"What were they doing at the DMV anyway?" Ray asked.

"Apparently they came to register a car gift to Nora," Adam responded.

"Oh!" Ray expressed surprise.

"What kind of car?" Kamal chimed in.

"That braggart told me that it was a baby Benz C class. I

don't know which specific type. All the while that he was talking to me, he was just showing off his stupid Rolex…"

Ray interjected, "Well, there is nothing really baby about a Mercedes Benz. His family must be quite rich. Is that the reason why Nora's mum wants her daughter married to this guy? I mean, it is obvious that she had that preference before she knew you are the competitor…"

Adam interjected, "It is Richard who is a baby. Money is not everything, and certainly, money does not translate into enduring happiness in marriage."

"I am sensing competition here. Can you smell it?" Kamal asked Ray and then remarked before Ray could respond. "My mistake. It was not a competition I smelled; it was jealousy."

Adam snarled at Kamal, "You must be out of your mind. Who is going to be jealous of a stupid young man? In fact, scratch the young from my last statement. He is just plain stupid. Just because he is younger and his father is richer, he drives a Mercedes S550 as a twenty-something-year-old, and wears a Rolex does not mean anything to me. His head may be in the clouds, but that is his problem, not mine."

I am still me
My watch does not define me
I wore my Casio computer watch
Until I got my Rolex watch
And I threw my Casio watch away

My car does not define me
I drove my lovely Kia Rio
Until I bought a Mercedes S550
And I got rid of the Kia Rio

My clothes do not define me
I happily wore my unknown brands
Until I got my Brooks Brothers
And I burned the unknown brands

My shoes do not define me
I looked good in whatever I wear

Until I got some Berluti shoes
And I threw my old shoes in the trash

Material wealth does not define me
It has only changed me
Not to someone else
But to someone who doesn't care

Kamal shook his head and remarked, "I actually agree with Adam. Just because somebody is younger does not mean that they are better than older folks."

Adam acknowledged Kamal's statement and agreed. He said, "There you go." He then noticed that Kamal elbowed Ray in a 'watch your hypocrite friend' gesture, so Adam realized that he had just been played by Kamal. Kamal was actually teasing Adam with respect to his preference for Nora over Aneida.

"The issue of Nora versus Aneida is totally different. In fact, there is no comparison at all." Adam tried to justify himself.

"Really?" Kamal questioned in disagreement. "Let us do the similarities and differences in the two interesting scenarios that you are in, shall we? Looking at issues from your view and looking at issues from Nora's view:

Your view: Aneida is old.

Nora's view: Adam is old.

Your view: Aneida has children from another marriage.

Nora's view: Adam has children from another marriage.

Your view: Nora is smoking hot.

Nora's view: Richard is smoking hot and rich."

"Richard is just smoking, and he will burn his face," Adam interjected quite unable to be patient while he was being ripped apart by Kamal's analogy.

"I think that the green-eyed monster called jealousy is back," Kamal expressed.

Adam did not tell his friends that when he got home and saw a couple of strands of grey hair on his head after his encounter with Richard Young, he quickly plucked them out with great swiftness like a horticulturist who suddenly discovered some weeds in the flower pot of his exotic plant. He removed another grey strand of hair from his beard to prevent it from 'contaminating' his remaining dark hair. 'Those grey hair were precocious,' he mumbled to himself at that time.

At present, Adam simply ignored Kamal and continued his ranting. "That spoiled brat should have introduced himself with the other four-letter nickname for Richard."

"Rich?" Kamal asked with sarcasm.

"C'mon!" Adam replied.

"Rick?" Kamal asked again with tongue in cheek.

"Seriously? Forget it." Adam waved his right hand to dismiss the conversation out of frustration.

"C'mon, Adam! Maybe it is fate that is trying to prevent you from suffering a massive heart attack from this chick," Kamal tried to find a positive spin on the disappointment Adam felt.

"You do not seem to get it. I really love Nora. If I get a heart attack from her, so be it. At least, I will die a very happy man," Adam concluded.

Me and You
I am serious about you
Like a major heart attack
I am attracted to you
Like a powerful magnet
I am drawn to you
Like the pull of gravity
I am destined to lodge with you
Like a saddle embolus

What do I have to do
To fully convince you
That truly I love you
And I am the right guy for you?

"Ok, I get it. You really love her, but you are facing a very stiff opposition from her mum that may be almost insurmountable for this young daisy," Kamal opined. "Moreover, your rival is…"

"He is not my rival," Adam interjected. "He doesn't stand a chance."

"But he has the mum's endorsement, and you know how powerful mothers are in these things," Kamal reasoned.

"I agree with you. My first task is to actually get Nora on my side completely. Then, I will work to get Zinnia on my side."

Loving you from one to ten

One
You are my number one
Nothing can change that

Two
I love you too
No circumstance can change that

Three
Our love will set us free
Nobody can change that

Four
Your love is what I am longing for
No one can change that

Five
For your hand do I strive
No human being can change that

Six
Your silence has put me in a fix
We need to change that

Seven
I want to be with you in heaven
We need to strive for that

Eight
Having eight children will be great
We need to start working on that

Nine
Your smile makes me feel fine
We need more of that

Ten
Loving you makes me the happiest of men
We need to solidify that

How?
By marrying me, darling, by marrying me!

"I know that you guys think that there is a rough and tough road ahead of me if I want to get to marriage promised land with Nora. However, let me reassure you that I can persevere," Adam expressed with confidence.

"I don't know who gave you the fake promise of a marriage promised land with Nora. Honestly, I do not want to sound pessimistic. However, if you will stand any remote chance, shouldn't she should be standing with you? Definitely, she should not be accepting the gift of an expensive car if she is absolutely not interested in the other guy," Kamal voiced his opinion.

"I am sure that there must be a reasonable explanation for it. Maybe her mum forced her to be with the guy. It was obvious to me that day that she was not happy with him," Adam rationalized.

Ray and Kamal looked at each other and shook their heads in amazement at the apparent lack of insight demonstrated by their smitten friend.

Kamal then remarked, "I think Adam will need divine intervention."

"I agree with you," Ray concurred.

"Remind me why I call you guys my friends," Adam responded.

"Because we are," Ray replied.

Adam shook his head, sighed, and remarked, "For the first time in my life, I really wish I was rich."

"You are. You are rich in your heart, just not in your wallet," Ray tried to cheer him up.

"I think our society discriminates against poor doctors," Adam opined. "Who am I kidding? Chicks will always prefer rich in the wallet rather than heart, maybe except Bonita."

"What did you mean? I am rich, and I was rich when she married me," Kamal defended himself.

"Really? You had no penny with Kandie cleaning you out," Adam tried to remind Kamal.

"My job paid $100, Kandie took $99. Uncle Sam took 75 cents. Therefore, I still had 25cents left. So, I had more than a penny when Bonita married me," Kamal argued in jest.

Adam raised his right hand and said, "Let me make you guys a promise from my heart."

"Don't make a promise that you will not be able to keep," Ray advised.

"I am certainly going to try," Adam emphasized.

"What is the stupid promise anyway?" Kamal inquired.

"If Nora marries me, I will do something really special, I will do everything I can for us to have a true honeymoon," Adam promised.

"And that is what is special?" Kamal queried.

"Yes. It will be really special. It will be like having our honeymoon on the moon."

Kamal chuckled and remarked, "While you are there, build a castle too." He then turned to Ray and asked, "Do you think he is still sane enough to practice medicine? I think he has gone bonkers!"

Adam ignored Kamal and continued. "I am very good at getting things done. I can be patient and persevere to win Nora. I know it. I have been through this path before."

"I am sure that you meant that you have a 'heart for breakdance' and not that you want a 'dance with heartbreak,' right?" Kamal asked Adam, hoping that he would be reasonable and come back to his senses.

"Look, guys. I can persevere. Did you think Eva gave me a chance the first time I talked to her as a medical student?

You have to realize that a medicine resident and a surgical resident were already drooling over her. Yet, in the end, she went for a loving, outstanding medical student. C'mon guys, I am good. I am confident in my skin. No lady will want to miss my package," Adam reiterated beaming with a smile which can best be described as masculine pride or ignorant over-confidence.

"Your package or your baggage? That was then bro, wake up! This is now," Kamal tried to jolt Adam to reality with his words.

"I heard you, but you have to remember that I am not like you. Unlike you that is getting old and withering, I am cheese. I am aging with grace while increasing in intense flavors. I am a diamond, my sparkle always stays. I am a river of love, and I continue to flow. I am indeed a rare breed, and I bring a lot of value. Furthermore, ladies want the guy who gets going when the going gets tough…like me."

Kamal wanted to respond. He opened his mouth and then closed it in despair as he shook his head.

Adam continued, "What? Look here Mr. Naysayer, when I first talked to Eva back in the days, some people like you thought I had zero chance too. I did not listen to them. I went to her, and I said 'Eva, how are you doing? There is a book by an African author by the name Ayi Kwei Armah. He wrote a novel in 1968 which he entitled *The Beautyful Ones Are Not Yet Born*. You know what babe, if Ayi Kwei Armah meets you, he will change the title to *The Beautyful One Has Now Been Born*, because she is here talking to me right now— you!"

Ray chuckled.

Adam smiled and continued, "Eva smiled initially and then remarked, 'thank you, but you are not my type.' and she wanted to walk away."

"My quick response shocked her, and it took her breath away!" Adam remarked, being proud of himself.

Ray and Kamal chuckled.

"So, what did you say, Mr. Reverse Loverboy,…em… em…Mr. Lover Oldman?" Ray asked.

Adam recalled his statement to Eva. "What type are you and

what type are you looking for? Baby, I am flexible, dependable, reliable, adaptable, and even my blood type is O positive. My dear, I am universal, pluripotent, but I want to be a committed stem cell, just for you Eva. I want to love you forever and ever."

Kamal smiled. Somehow, he looked impressed with Adam's move on Eva but quickly shrugged it off.

Adam continued to relish in his recalls. "Later on, during her birthday, I gave her a real flower this time. Of course, no more plastic flowers. I do pay attention too...you know..."

"Yeah. You are really special," Kamal interjected.

"Yes. Wait... special? Retarded special or just awesome special?" Adam sought clarification.

"No comment," Kamal replied.

"I gave her an edible, but symbolic gift and a beautiful card which I think had a flowery landscape or maybe a rose or something like that."

"What did you mean by 'symbolic gift?'" Ray interjected while making air quotes on mentioning 'symbolic gift.'

"I gave a box of mac n cheese that has 'made with real cheese' written on it, and I remarked in my card that I might be cheesy, but babe, I am real, and I am for real," Adam replied. "Believe me, she prominently displayed my card at her birthday party. After that, other students started thinking of her as my girl. The other competitors, including the obviously senior, richer, more educated post-graduate trainees, got the memo to back off, that Eva is already where she belongs...in my arms."

"Cheap," Kamal remarked.

"Astute," Adam countered.

"That was then," Kamal responded.

"Then, now, and forever," Adam replied.

"Kids!" Ray chimed in to stop the back and forth between Adam and Kamal.

"My point is that Adam needs to get his priorities right. The lady he loves is dating a younger richer guy, and the one who loves him is not quite acceptable to him yet because he is still keeping his ray of hope at twilight," Kamal expressed.

"Maybe he just needs some time," Ray tried to defend Adam.

"Yes. Time is what he needs, but time is also what he doesn't have. The way he is going, he is going to need to get himself a mail order bride eventually," Kamal asserted.

"C'mon, Kamal! Nobody does mail order any more. It is internet age baby," Ray corrected Kamal with tongue in cheek.

"Yes, old-timer! There is something called the internet now," Adam suggested to Kamal.

"Well, feel free to dilly dally as you want," Kamal responded. He then faced Ray and addressed him. "Your love-crazy brother here is in love with a lady he can't get, and he is moving away from the lady he can get."

Ray then faced Adam and remarked, "You are in emotional trouble my friend. Option one was rejected, and option two was not acceptable. What are you going to do?"

Before Adam could respond to this pseudo-rhetorical question, Kamal chimed, "He can order a wife on Amazon, you know, the internet Amazon, not the river in Brazil. However, if you want to get a pretty mermaid from the Amazon river in the jungle itself, you can actually get one that will be a tropical bombshell. She will be amazing. You just have to type in your nature which is 'Hard To Tease and Please then slash, slash in Wild Wild West....'"

Adam looked at Ray while looking puzzled. "What exactly is this fake genius talking about?"

Kamal responded "Silly old-timer! That is how you search for things on the internet. It is the meaning of http\\www."

"No internet wife for me anyway. I don't really agree with getting a wife abroad except if you are totally out of options, or you are convinced that she is your soulmate." Adam replied.

"What do you mean?" Ray asked.

"I have heard a lot of stories from international medical graduates when we were in medical residency training who wanted to marry from their countries of origin because they erroneously thought that those ladies would be more attuned to their cultures. Their assumption was that such a lady would be different from their stereotype of the typical

American woman. Great mistake! One of the doctors told me that he felt that as soon as the lady landed, and made it to Dulles Airport access road, she was already telling him that she is an American now and she knows her rights. The shocker for him was that the wife had not even reached the main highway I-495 yet. The poor guy said he felt used. The worst part was that her father was a friend of his family. Personally, I don't think that ladies abroad are going to be any different from US born ladies so long as they live here with you, and they will surely live here with you because what then will be the essence of marriage if they remain abroad after being married?" Adam explained.

After a moment of awkward silence, Kamal remarked, "Nora is doing everything in a polite manner to tell you *no,* but you are still pursuing her. The issue here regarding Nora is North to South, but here you are going to the East.

Adam replied, "That tells you that I am wise. I just need to be patient."

"How could that possibly be wisdom when the issue is North and South. This means that her North is *yes, I don't love you enough and I don't want you,* and her South is *no, I will still not marry you if you are the last man on earth plus mum will refuse anyway.* Yet, here you are, heading to the East in blindfolds," Kamal questioned.

"The East is where wisdom is a brother. Remember, even in ancient times, the most famous wisemen in history, all three of them, came from the East. So, if I am going East when you, a non-wiseman, is going North or South, then I am just following the footsteps of my predecessor wisemen," Adam rationalized.

"Stop trying to be a wisecracker. I think you are just infatuated with Nora. Maybe because she is young and beautiful," Kamal opined.

"Believe me when I tell you this. Nora is not the most beautiful lady I have seen. It is just that I am drawn to her like a magnet, and I really love her for reasons that I cannot fully explain."

Knowing what to know

How do I make you realize,
That being with you, I always fantasize?
How do I make you aware,
That with me, you have nothing to fear?
How do I make it clear,
That to me, you'll always be dear?
How do I make it obvious,
That to me, you'll always be precious?
How do I make you understand,
That you make my heart expand?
How do I make you know,
That you make my heart overflow?
How do I make you see,
That you are the comfort I seek?

I know that it is true
That I truly love you
But how to convince you
Hmmm!, I don't have a clue

"Of course, you don't have a clue. You are really clueless. She has given you all the clues you need. You seemed to want everything spelled out in layman terms. Are you sure that you are a real doctor? I mean, doctors are supposed to be smart people," Kamal queried.

"You can go and ask my professors in the medical school," Adam replied.

Kamal shook his head and remarked, "I am sure that they are looking for you. They probably want to withdraw their diploma. On a serious note, I will hate to see you hurt. I really do hope you wake up to reality very soon."

"In case you have not noticed, I am not sleeping," Adam retorted.

Ray interrupted them and remarked. "Ok guys, I may have to give both of you a time out if you don't cut it out. Both of you are just quibbling like toddlers that you are."

"You should tell your old friend here. He is the one babbling like a baby, trying to go on a fantasy voyage," Kamal advised.

"I will not dignify that comment with a response," Adam responded.

"You make it sound as if you love Nora like Romeo loved Juliet," Kamal observed.

"I love Nora more than Romeo loved Juliet," Adam asserted.

"Your proof?" Kamal asked.

"In my heart," Adam responded.

"We can't see it. You have an invisible love—it can be felt but cannot be seen or touched," Ray chimed in.

"Yeah! He has an invisible, phantom, and at best, a one-sided love," Kamal agreed.

"I have an invincible love for Nora. It cannot be destroyed even by naysayers like you," Adam emphasized.

"Yeah. Fantasy love. Nothing but popcorn love. Your love affair with Nora is a mirage which only you can see," Kamal explained.

"That is your deluded opinion. In my Romeo and Juliet love affair, I think I should call mine a Romero and Julia love affair, Romero actually married Julia and they lived happily ever after," Adam related.

"You and your fantasy," Kamal opined.

Adam tried to look very serious and remarked, "I think I should make a mega movie about Romero and Julia. The movie will be *The Indomitable Love*. It will be a true story of unrelenting love, a true masterpiece starring Adam Gray as Romero, Nora Ahsan as Julia, Ray as a true friend indeed, and Kamal Brown as himself, the evil uncle Naysayer."

Kamal simply shook his head.

"How did the Romero and Julia play go?" Ray asked Adam while playing along.

Adam cleared his throat to relate the story of unblemished love first heard by human ears and first known to human hearts according to him. This made Kamal roll his eyeballs like a teenager.

Adam continued, "Romero saw Julia, and he was mesmerized by her beauty and her demeanor. He was carried away by her gentle nature, her stunning beauty, her infectious smile and how she made him feel on top of the world. They finally got married and flew away together on Pegasus. They lived happily ever after in Paradise."

"What a depressing fairy tale," Kamal remarked.

"Remember that Nora's mum actually chewed me up at the dinner, asking me why I was feverishly fighting furiously for a forbidden fantasy?" Adam reminded his friends.

"That was a nice alliteration," Ray observed.

"The truth is that I really love Nora. Our relationship may sound like a fairy tale, but that does not mean that it is not real," Adam concluded.

Fairy tales

From Snow White to Cinderella
Dealing with the evil stepmother
From Rapunzel to Jack to the beauty
Dealing with salad, beans, and rose
From Tarzan to the little mermaid
Dealing with wildlife exploration
From the frog prince to Shrek's Fiona
Dealing with the kiss from a true love
Fairy tales are sweet tales

They typically meet in an unusual situation
The prince meets the princess
They face challenges
But in the end
They overcome the challenges
And they live happily ever after.

Loving you has been like a fairy tale
We came from lands far far away
Traveled across the sea
Journeyed over an expanse of land
And we are going to the land beyond beyond
To live happily ever after in Paradise

Such is what I am hoping for
Such is what I am itching for
Such is what I am yearning for

Such is what I am longing for
Such is what I am praying for

If this is fantasy,
It is surely fantastic.
Baby, be mine.
I love you.

"I still can't understand why you keep looking away from Aneida," Kamal questioned.

"She is over 40 years old now. That is really old, I mean, very old for a woman, and she has baggage," Adam expressed.

"But you are older than her, and you have baggage too, Mr. Hypocrite," Kamal argued.

Adam ignored Kamal's comment and continued. "Moreover, there may be issues with respect to step-children with Aneida, but it is a fresh start with Nora."

"Fresh start for who? For you or for Nora? Is Nora not going to be dealing with step-children issues too if she marries you?" Kamal asked Adam in an attempt to point out his hypocrisy again.

There was never a time that Adam would see Nora without him melting like butter on a breakfast toast. When she smiles and talks to him, his heart melts faster than burning a candle at both ends. It is not possible for Nora to ever understand how much Adam loves her. She really cannot understand that his heart goes bonkers over her, from morning to night.

Adam related that he tried to make his unrelenting love clear to Nora about two weeks ago when he bumped into her at the Alexandria Mall. Fortunately for him, she was alone. He recalled that he did not hold back. "Nora, my love for you is part of me like my shadow. The fact that I close my eyes does not mean that it is gone. All I have done since the last time I saw you was close my eyes. I still really love you. It is futile for me to deny it, as it will just be as if I am trying to run away from my shadow. You complement me, you are part of me, and I will always love and care about you. I think about you all the time. I long for you all the time."

"Please leave me alone," Nora replied with a broken voice. She looked down in order to avoid making eye contact with Adam, but she did not make any attempt to walk away.

Immeasurable love
The weight of my love for you
Cannot be measured in pounds
The length of my love for you
Cannot be measured in yards
The height of my love for you
Cannot be measured in feet
The volume of my love for you
Cannot be measured in fluid ounces
The depth of my love for you
Cannot be measured by echo sounder
The quantity of my love for you
Cannot be measured at all
The quality of my love for you
Cannot be assessed at all

My love for you can only be evaluated
My desire for you can only be expressed
My feelings for you can only be related
My care about you can only be explained
My longing for you can only be conveyed
From my heart to your heart

When will you be ready to know?
When do you want to be in the know?
How much I miss you
How much I love you

So, Adam walked around her and said, "Tell me you love Richard and that you will rather be with him, and I promise to leave you alone."

Nora did not reply, but she did not walk away. She stared transfixed at the same spot, just looking down, trying desperately not to make eye contact with Adam.

State of affairs
I know that you are not a fool
You know that seeing you makes me drool
So, there is no need to pretend
I want us to be more than friends

My love for you
I can never ignore
My passion for you
I never felt before

Being with you
Makes me feel so blessed
Being away from you
Makes me feel depressed

I think about you
All day long
I dream of you
All night long

Marry me, please
I am on my knees

Adam then remarked, "Then try and explain to your mum that you love me."

"Did you think that I didn't try?" Nora asked Adam with tear laden eyes inadvertently making eye contact.

"I am so sorry," Adam responded almost moved to tears himself.

Nora was now drying her tears. Intense pain was written boldly on her face. "I am sorry, but I need to go." She finally mustered. With a gloomy face, she lowered her head, kept her chin down, and remarked, "I am so sorry Adam, but please leave me alone."

"And she left," Adam concluded. "My head went blank for a while. I don't know how long I stood at the same spot after she left."

"What next?" Ray asked Adam.

"I feel as if I am losing Nora. Unfortunately, Nora may be gradually leaving my grasp, but she is still in my head, and the feelings I have for her is still growing in my heart. That is my major problem."

Part Three

Prized Possession:
The story of Kamal

Part Three: Section One: What I Have

"Hope things worked out better for you, my friend!" Ray remarked, facing Kamal.

"I wish that was completely true. Things got better. Then, things got worse, much worse. I am not sure if things are still in the worse phase or they are gradually going into the worst phase right now," Kamal replied looking dejected.

'What happened?" Ray pressed him

"I don't even know where to start, my brother. I don't know. All I know is that I can use some good news right now. Any good news will be great!" Kamal replied with a sigh.

"What really happened?" Ray inquired again. "Did things get worse with Kandie?" he asked without waiting for a response to his initial question.

"A lot happened, my friend. I mean, things got a lot worse with Kandie. She is the real problem. She is a pain in the neck, in the butt, in the—I mean, she is a bad pain everywhere. Unfortunately, things are quite challenging with Bonita right now too."

"I am sorry to hear that," Adam remarked.

"Kandie is a major problem, but she is easier for me to handle in a way. What gets to me is the sadness of Bonita. It is as if she is on edge all the time now. I fear that her joy has been replaced by anxiety."

Ray and Adam looked at each other with pity for Kamal written on their faces in bold letters. After a moment of awkward silence, Kamal began to relate his tale of woes since the last time he saw his friends.

"Remember that during our discussions, our strategy to counter Kandie's seductive plan was to get Bonita on my side when I am making those visits to see my son," Kamal recalled.

"Yes, that is true! Did it work?" Adam inquired.

"That strategy was like packing a suitcase in a hurry when you are struggling not to miss your flight at the airport. After you closed the suitcase, then you realized that you forgot to include something important, so you open the suitcase and repack. You close the suitcase thinking you are finally done, only for you see that something else was sticking out. This makes you open the suitcase again and push it in, only for something else to be sticking out from the other side...much to your chagrin and painful disappointment."

"C'mon, Kamal, enough of philosophy! What happened?" Ray asked impatiently as he wanted Kamal to cut through the chase.

"Well, Kandie and Bonita fought!" Kamal reported as he sunk his head into his hands on the table.

"What!" Adam and Ray exclaimed in unison.

"No, they did not fight with their fists, but believe me they are fighting with everything else right now," Kamal explained. "A lot of it was my fault. I was too naïve. I erroneously thought that they would get along. How wrong I was!"

"How so?" Adam asked, being surprised at Kamal's statement.

"I did not quite appreciate how low Kandie was willing to stoop and how determined she is to ruin my marriage to Bonita so that she can stand a chance to get back with me," Kamal lamented.

"That is very serious," Ray remarked as he patted Kamal on his shoulder in an 'I am here for you' gesture.

Kamal continued. "On the issue of getting Bonita to go

with me anytime I wanted to see Junior, it was tough for me largely because I did not know how best to bring it up. Bonita and I have been married for three years, and we do not have any child yet, and she is now 33 years old. Hitherto, if this bothered her, she did not show it. Honestly, I was quite happy so long as we are together child or no child, I didn't care. I love Bonita. She is the best of what I have going for me. Now, Kandie has ruined that blissful innocence for me through her actions," Kamal lamented.

Ray and Adam kept quiet, giving Kamal the opportunity to calm down and gather his thoughts.

"Bonita and I normally take a leisure walk together on Saturday and Sunday mornings before breakfast. The walk was our pastime together outside the house. Sometimes we do light jogs as well. We just talk and appreciate nature and things around us. Believe me, sometimes we will walk two miles on the trail, and then walk back to our car, making four miles of gentle walking lasting less than an hour and a half."

"That's nice," Adam remarked. "I need to find a way to exercise more often."

"Choose a wife who likes the other type of exercise, and you will get your muscles contracting and your heart pumping too. You are bound to achieve the same thing," Ray surmised.

"You really have problems," Adam responded to Ray.

Kamal continued. "Those walks are great. Time and distance go by quickly when you are with somebody you love and who reciprocates your affection. One day, during one of those walk sessions, there was a woman in the park whose son was having a really bad day. The little boy was incalcitrant and was throwing a javelin-like tantrum, annoying everybody with his incessant cry. When we passed by them, I made a funny face at him and waived. Surprisingly, he looked at me with a puzzled expression, and he stopped crying. We were surprised. So, I went over to him with Bonita, and I shook his hand with the mother looking on, feeling relieved that this little boy stopped crying, even if for a minute. I introduced myself to him and asked him his name. He took my hand, and his mother told me that his name is Frederick. I told him to relax and give mummy a break. I then snapped his fingers which made him giggle. So, I did it again, and he wanted me to keep doing it. I ended up teaching Bonita, Frederick's mum, and his adolescent brother Frank how to snap the finger."

"How do you snap a finger?" Ray inquired.

Kamal shook Ray's hands and snapped his finger. Ray asked him to do it again so that he could understand it and practice it too.

Kamal then continued, "Later that afternoon, when we were watching TV, I placed my head on Bonita's lap. She recalled the event earlier that morning and remarked that I was good with kids. Then, quite fortuitously, she asked if I missed my son. It was the opportunity that I needed. I confirmed to her that I did miss him and would love to actually spend more time with him if it was possible. However, I reassured her that I am quite happy that we have each other."

Truly Special
The infectious smile
The calming voice
The welcoming hug
The supporting presence
The reassuring handholding
The soothing pat
The playful tap
The loving embrace
The breathtaking kiss and
The terrific touchy tango

Baby, you are as cute as can be
Sweetie, you are as pretty as can be
Honey, you are as beautiful as can be
Darling, you are everything to me.

Nothing can change that fact.

I love you

"Bonita voiced understanding, but she insisted that I should also spend more time with my son. She told me to bring him around so that she can meet him. It was my prayer-that-has-been-answered moment because I could then invite Kandie and Junior to my home, get them introduced, and Bonita can be my unsuspecting bodyguard."

When Kamal informed Kandie that he would love for her and junior to meet Bonita and he can resume his visitations, Kandie was happy and looked forward to the meeting.

To Kamal, it was an opportunity to bury the hatchet with Kandie, while making it clear to her that it was over between them. Contacts between them will be only about their son. There is never going to be 'Kandie and Kamal' or 'candy and caramel,' the sweet couple anymore. That chapter has closed and its coffin nailed and buried. Indeed, that was a dead tale buried in the annals of time in the magistrate court where Kandie and her lawyer put up a show of shame a few years ago.

To Bonita, meeting Kamal junior would surely make her loving husband happy. The unwritten universal law also states that if you are merciful to somebody else's child, your own child will be on hand to receive mercy from others too. She definitely would love to have a son of her own too.

To Kandie, getting to meet Bonita was the best thing that could happen. It would give her the very necessary opportunity to size up and assess her competitor. It would give her the chance to study her, know what makes her tick, and understand what made Kamal love her; and she will then figure out how to crush her competitor. As far as Kandie was concerned, Bonita needs to go and find her own husband elsewhere. Kandie and Kamal belong together like the nut and bolt. Yes, sometimes the nut can be separated from the bolt, but they still have to come together for optimum function. Kandie then mused to herself, "Kamal is the bolt and I am the nut. We belong together," as she accepted the invitation to bring Kamal junior to Kamal's home the following Saturday.

The following Saturday, Kandie knocked on the door to Kamal's single-family home. She was in phase one of her "win back my husband" plan. When Kamal opened the door for her, he was visibly stunned. This was supposed to be a simple family meet and greet, but Kandie appeared dressed for a formal dinner with the president of a country. She looked incredibly gorgeous. Her blue gown had beautiful embroideries. Her shoes were elegant, and they matched her dress perfectly. She wore a shiny necklace that was screaming, "I am very expensive." There was something familiar about the necklace, and momentarily, Kamal recognized it. He gave it to her as a gift of love on their wedding night. Obviously, Kandie wanted to remind Kamal of their love even though she is visiting Bonita on her turf. This scared Kamal a bit, but this fear disappeared as Kamal junior lovingly hugged him at that auspicious moment. He was well dressed too, in a Navy-blue suit and white satin shirt with a royal-blue bow tie. Kamal picked him up and walked into the house to a smiling Bonita, who took Junior from her husband, giving him a warm embrace. She then put him down and went over to Kandie as Kamal stammered with the introduction.

"Bonita, this is Kandie. Kandie, meet Bonita, my wife." Kamal added my wife deliberately to establish who is his wife, without a doubt. In his mind, he said, "Bonita my wife, meet Kandie, my child's mother." He hoped that introducing them that way firmly established his relationship with them and would be enough to keep Kandie at bay. In reality, Kamal was still apprehensive of Kandie. He tried to reassure himself that Bonita is the same age as Kandie and she definitely can hold her ground against her. However, there was just something odd in the back of his head that was constantly telling him to be wary of Kandie. He shrugged off the idea that Kandie came to his home to harm Bonita as he walked his son to the living room while Kandie and Bonita continued to exchange pleasantries. He took a surreptitious glance at the two ladies in and out of his life and concluded to himself that they seem to be getting along well. This was what Kamal hoped for and preferred. Now, it was the reality, and this made Kamal smile.

Kandie brought Bonita a gift of beautiful well-packed female beauty products with chocolate. She also brought a dish to share with her hosts, claiming that she was raised to always bring a dish whenever she was invited to dinner while expressing a fake apology for doing so to Bonita. When Kamal realized that Kandie had brought his favorite dish of spaghetti and meatballs in marinara sauce, he knew it was a message to him. It was crystal clear to him that Kandie was lying, but what could he do other than to go along with it at that point?

After initial appetizers of unending tacos and fresh organic salsa and fruit drinks, while they were chatting and watching the reruns of a popular sitcom, they finally settled down to eat the sumptuous Mexican-style dinner prepared by Bonita. The array of food included corn on the cob *Elote*, a trifecta of fish, chicken and beef *enchiladas*, and the twenty-three ingredients rusty red *mole poblano* sauce served over turkey with rice and vegetables. The meal was so delicious that Kamal junior's satin white shirt became multi-colored from all the stains from different foods. This was much to the delight of Bonita who saw her husband's child enjoying himself, and much to the suppressed anger of Kandie who realized that her son seemed to connect well with Bonita and appeared to genuinely like her. Kandie could not readily make up her mind whether it was a good thing or a bad thing that her son felt at home with Bonita. On the one hand, this is good because he is at home with his father and Bonita will take good care of him, but on the other hand, Bonita is her rival. Bonita snatched Kamal from her. Bonita has no business in their lives. It was supposed to be Kandie and Kamal, the sweet couple and their sweet child. Kandie quickly snapped out of her thought when she realized that her demeanor was changing and did not want to give her strategy away too easily. "After all, this is a marathon, not a sprint. This is a full-scale war, not a skirmish," Kandie convinced herself. She reassured herself that she has to remain strategic to win the war with Bonita and get her husband back.

Kandie forced a smile and insisted that she would like them to try her dish too. At least, they should have a taste. She knew that it was Kamal's favorite dish. Unfortunately, Kamal never mentioned to Bonita that spaghetti with meatballs was his favorite meal with Kandie and that her marinara sauce was to die for. He shook his head, realizing that it would be the worst moment and place to reveal such information. Unfortunately, Bonita was quite unsuspecting, and she commented that the sauce tastes great and asked if Kandie would like to share the recipe with her. This gave Kamal goosebumps, but he tried to maintain his cool and simply smiled.

At the conclusion of the visitation, Bonita gave Kamal Junior a Lego City Monster Truck toy while Kamal gave him a Ferrari Radio Remote Control car. Kamal and Bonita then escorted Kandie and Junior to the driveway to get into Kandie's car. Kamal picked up his son and gave him a big hug despite all the multi-colored food stains on his clothes. The sight of the father hugging his son lovingly had a tremendous effect on both Kandie and Bonita, albeit in different ways. For Bonita, more than ever, she wants to have a child for Kamal. She wants a family complete with children. For Kandie, more than ever, the reality is that she needs to get rid of Bonita so that she can have her family back together. The sooner she can get rid of Bonita, the better. Time is of the essence. It would be a lot easier to get rid of Bonita when there are no children involved in her fake temporary marriage to Kamal. After all, Kandie is the sweet candy who should bring sweetness to Kamal's life.

Two weeks later, Kandie came to Kamal's home to drop Junior off so that he could spend the whole day with Kamal and Bonita. They had agreed to take the joint custody arrangement gradually in a step-up manner till they reach their goal when Junior could spend alternate weekends with

Kamal. Kamal took his son into the yard to play catch with a soft toy football while Kandie and Bonita were discussing on the porch. Occasionally, Kamal would look towards the women, as he was leery of anything untoward happening between them, but nothing happened. They just talked—or so it seemed to Kamal. After some time, Kandie drove off. The plan was for her to return around seven p.m. to take Junior home that day.

They continued this increasing length of father-son "get together" for about two months when Kandie suggested that Kamal could come and pick Junior up and let him stay with him for the three-day Martin Luther King junior birthday holiday weekend. Kamal was very happy to hear this, and Bonita was also excited about the idea. Kandie then suggested that Kamal should stop by on his way from work to pick his son on Friday. She promised to get him ready as soon as he gets back from school. Kamal saw this as a golden opportunity to spend quality time with his son and was very happy. He informed Bonita, and she was very excited too. They both looked forward to it. Bonita was particularly elated that they would finally have a child in their home for the first time. Although not her own biological child, he is family. They bought many decorative child-friendly things into the third bedroom in their house where junior would be staying anytime he would come over. They painted the walls in different shades of beautiful blue colors, having learned that blue is junior's favorite color. Bonita's formal education as an early childhood educator was in full display as she bought a lot of brain-stimulating fun games that they could play together with junior over that long weekend. She also planned an outing for them at *Kids Forever*, an indoor games and sports arcade that targets children and adolescents, in Falls Church, Virginia.

Kamal was so excited to pick his son up on Friday afternoon as agreed upon that he decided to leave work early. He called Kandie from work that he was on his way. Kandie busied herself monitoring when Kamal was set to arrive and would occasionally look through her window overlooking the parking spaces in front of her apartment complex. When she saw Kamal's car pull into one of the visitor's spaces, Kandie got really excited and ready. Her plan was now ready for implementation. She let her transparent nightgown hang loosely, applied her perfume, and adjusted her *Wonderbra* to reveal her treasures without exposing them. She was ready. Today is the day. She had sent her cousin to take junior out for ice cream with a stern instruction to keep junior engaged for at least three hours. He should only come back at eight p.m. giving her enough time to complete her plan for Kamal and achieve her objective.

When Kandie heard that familiar pattern of knocking on her door, she had a loving sinister smile on her face as she quickly looked at herself in the mirror for the umpteenth time. However, before she could reply in the "hard to resist" stimulating voice that she knew always turn Kamal on like a television set, she suddenly heard a somewhat familiar female voice at the door as well. There was no doubt that the tepid military-style knocking was from Kamal, but who was talking to him? Kandie asked herself as she tried to quickly process whose voice she heard. Her heart jumped into her mouth when it dawned on her that it was Bonita's voice she heard. She quickly tip-toed to the door and peeped through the 'peephole' on the door to have a visual confirmation that the voice she heard was truly Bonita's. When she saw Bonita smiling next to Kamal at the door, Kandie was filled with rage. Why did he bring her along? Why did he decide to ruin her perfect plan? "What sort of nonsense is this?" Kandie asked herself. "He did not mention that he was coming with this woman," Kandie's anger continued to increase as she quickly dashed to her bedroom to hurriedly change into a regular dress. Kandie was very angry, but she tried not to show it as she opened the door for Kamal and Bonita.

Unknown to Kandie, when Kamal was about thirty minutes away from Kandie's apartment, it dawned on him that he was never to go and see Kandie by himself in her apartment. He, therefore, made a quick turn off the I-95 beltway and called Bonita that he is on his way home to pick her. He explained to Bonita that he feels that both of them should go to Kandie's apartment to pick Junior. He related to her that it would be a good gesture for her to reciprocate Kandie's visits. Furthermore, after taking Junior, the three of them can go to a restaurant that night for dinner. Since Bonita just came from work herself and had not started cooking dinner, it was a perfect plan. So, she got ready for him to pick her up to go to Kandie's place of abode.

Kandie tried to hide her disappointment and anger that Kamal had brought Bonita along. She complained that it was taking too long for her cousin who took Junior out briefly to come back. She asked them to wait a bit for her cousin while ushering Kamal and Bonita into their seats in the living room. Then she openly expressed being genuinely disappointed in Kamal for bringing Bonita along without first informing her that he was going to do so. In spinning the conversation, she expressed that she would have been better prepared for her to make her feel welcome and at home. This came to Bonita as a surprise with her observation of how perfect everything in Kandie's apartment looked. Even if she was expecting a visit from the president of the world, she couldn't have been more prepared. Bonita was convinced that something was odd; she just couldn't lay a finger on what it was. It was her sixth sense. Perhaps, if she were spiderwoman, her spider senses would be tingling.

Kandie subsequently excused herself from her guests in order to go and get her phone in the bedroom to call her cousin to bring Junior back now that his father had arrived. Bonita felt she interrupted something with her presence. Kamal noticed that Kandie was picking flower petals on the floor on her way to the bedroom and realized that the advice of his friends had worked. However, he pretended that nothing strange had happened. All of a sudden, Bonita leaned over to Kamal and in a soft voice asked him a question that he was not prepared for.

"Are you here for the child or the mum?" Bonita asked Kamal.

> **Author's note:** To my male readers, ladies have a way of studying and understanding other ladies when they are being mischievous. For us as guys, we just cannot understand it, and probably, we will never understand it!

Kamal was dumbfounded, but he had a quick recovery and retorted, "If I came here for the mum, do you think that I will drive all the way home to pick you and asked you to come here with me?"

"That's true," Bonita responded. "However, I don't think Kandie meant well."

Kamal did not respond.

For the first time in their marriage, Bonita made a firm negative suggestion to her husband that was almost a command. "I think she is trying something sinister. I am sorry, but I don't think you should be coming here to see Junior. Maybe, anytime you need to pick Junior up, you should arrange to meet in a public place away from here."

Kamal did not respond.

After Kandie finished her phone call with her cousin with 'a change of plan' message, she came to join Kamal and Bonita. She continued to complain that Kamal brought Bonita along without informing her and thereby, deprived her of the opportunity to adequately reciprocate Bonita's hospitality.

About an hour later, Junior returned with Kandie's cousin. Soon afterward, Kamal, Bonita, and Junior left. Having Junior at home brought out the maternal instinct in Bonita. She really enjoyed the company of her husband's son and truly wished that he was her son too. Unfortunately, they had to give him back to his mother on Monday evening. Bonita truly wished to have a child of her own.

Two weeks later, with the football frenzy in high gear in anticipation of the Superbowl, it was Kamal's turn to host Junior. He was elated that he could watch at least some of the Superbowl with his son. The plan was for him to meet Kandie and Junior in a park. He intended to go with Bonita to pick Junior up. However, Bonita's mum slipped and fell down the stairs at home in El Paso and broke her hip. This emergency made Bonita travel to El Paso to see her mum in the University of El Paso Medical Center. Therefore, Kamal had to go by himself to Watkins Neighborhood Park in Upper Marlboro to meet Kandie and pick his son up as planned. Kamal decided to play catch with his son using a kiddie football. While Kamal was trying to retrieve the ball after Junior had thrown it down a slope, he slipped on ice and fell, hitting his head on the root of a tree. He lost consciousness. Junior saw him fell. He cried aloud attracting the attention of Kandie who was already trying to make her way to her car to leave. When she turned, she saw her son running down a slope and fall. She quickly turned and ran towards him. Fortunately, he was not hurt. Kandie then saw Kamal further down the slope where he laid motionless with blood around his head, and she screamed for help which attracted bystanders. She called 9-1-1 for the emergency response team to come to their aid.

Within a few minutes, the loud siren of an ambulance filled the air. When the emergency medical technicians arrived at the scene, they went to Kamal who was now slightly coming around but was bleeding from his scalp.

"What happened?" Edward, the emergency medical technician, asked Kandie.

"My son was playing with his father over there. He slipped, fell down the slope, and passed out after hitting his head," Kandie responded.

"What is his name?" Edward inquired as he applied a dressing gauze to Kamal's head in an attempt to stop the bleeding.

"Kamal Brown," Kandie replied and also informed Edward of Kamal's date of birth.

"What is your name ma'am?" Edward asked Kandie.

"My name is Kandie, K-A-N-D-I-E. Kandie Brown. Is he going to be OK?" Kandie responded.

"I am sorry mam, but we need to take him to the Emergency Room of Greater Community Hospital, about two miles from here, for further evaluation and treatment."

Edward continued to document his assessment while the other technicians strapped Kamal onto the gurney and put him in the back of the ambulance. Kandie was watching him write his notes and noted that Edward wrote in his note that Kandie was the informant. However, in the section of the relationship of the informant to the patient, Edward wrote, *wife* without asking Kandie of her relationship with Kamal.

Kandie wondered whether she should correct him or not, but she liked seeing her name being written as *wife* to Kamal. She smiled and then quickly changed her demeanor to that of concern and repeated her question, "Is he going to be OK?"

"We hope for the best ma'am," Edward replied.

Kandie drove behind the ambulance to the hospital. In the hospital, she introduced herself as Kandie Brown and showed the hospital personnel her driver's license. Apparently, she never changed her name back to her maiden name. She put her name down as his wife and by default, his next of kin in the intake forms. In a bold move, Kandie put a restriction on phone calls and visitation to Kamal such that she is the only one who can call and visit him. She cited security and privacy concerns. She instructed the hospital that Kamal's name should not be listed in the hospital's patient directory. She switched Kamal's phone off and informed hospital staff that her husband needed to rest and did not want people to be bothering him with phone calls while he is recuperating. It was determined that Kamal had suffered a moderate concussion. His scalp laceration was sutured, but he was admitted to the neurological unit for close observation and further testing.

After waiting for two days without getting any response from Kamal and her calls automatically going into voicemail on his phone, Bonita was visibly disturbed. She had called the house phone landline multiple times as well without any pickup. She called their neighbor who stated that she has not seen Kamal come into the house and did not notice the front porch being lit the previous day. In her desperation, Bonita called Kandie trying to inquire about her husband since the last conversation Kamal had with her after dropping her off at the airport was to pick Junior up from Kandie at the park. However, Kandie did not answer the call and did not respond to any of the voicemail messages Bonita left her. This lack of information was particularly devastating for Bonita. She knew that something terrible must have happened to her husband. Kamal was not the type of man who would not have called to inquire about her and the wellbeing of her mum who had just endured a grueling three hours of orthopedic surgery to fix her broken hip. She made multiple calls to the area hospitals and the emergency medical services hotline without success. Therefore, she excused herself and took a return flight back from El-Paso, cutting her trip short. When she arrived, Kamal's car was not in the garage at home. She, therefore, proceeded to the police station to file a missing person complaint. When she mentioned that his car was also missing, the police detective entered the car information into their database and noted that the car was towed from Watkins Park having been left unattended for more than 24 hours, and it had violated parking rules by affecting street cleaning efforts. Bonita was distraught. The detective then gave her the news that Kamal had a head injury and was taken to the Greater Community Hospital. Bonita felt some sense of relief on hearing this, but her joy soon turned into profound anger when the officer added that Kamal was taken to the hospital in the company of his wife and son after the fall.

"But I am his wife," Bonita yelled.

"I am sorry ma'am. According to the report on file, it stated that his wife was at the scene," the detective explained.

Bonita was raging with fury, and she mumbled a heartfelt *thank you* to the police detective as she dashed out of the police station to her car and drove immediately to the Greater Community Hospital. After a lengthy process of identifying herself and establishing her relationship with Kamal, she was informed of his hospital room number. When she got there, she saw Kandie at the door of the room, having just returned from the Nurses' station where she had gone to request some ice. A loud verbal altercation ensued immediately between Bonita and Kandie which could have resulted in fistfights but for the quick response of the nursing staff and prompt alert and response of the security personnel. Despite the physical restraining of Kandie and Bonita from each other, they continued to trade insults.

"You are a deplorable human being! What did you do to my husband?" Bonita accused Kandie.

"You are a husband snatcher! Leave my husband and our son alone. Go and find your own husband," Kandie responded.

"You are an evil omen. You are evil and rotten to the core. That explains why they give candy at Halloween."

"Kamal is my man and the father of our child. I don't know where he found you or what he is doing with someone like you?"

"He found a better alternative where you left him. You threw a good man away, and now you think the world revolves around your finger."

"I suffered for him. I suffered with him. I have been with him from college through thick and thin. We went through all our challenges together, and now that he is okay and well to do, you have come to reap the fruit of my toil," Kandie claimed.

"What suffering did you suffer for him? Ripping his heart out in court while calling him an abusive husband? You knew that was not a truthful allegation. Is your being with him through thick and thin the shameful 'We are the winners; I am wild and free' tee shirt you wore in court?"

Kandie was surprised that Bonita knew all these details. Nonetheless, she pressed on.

"I do not have time for this nonsense out of your mouth. Our family is me, Kamal and our son. So, do yourself a favor and go away when there may still be a loser out there who may be interested in marrying you," Kandie remarked as she was being led away from the neurology ward by the hospital's security personnel.

Bonita was weeping uncontrollably as she finally made her way into Kamal's room who was still sleeping from the effect of the medications that were administered by his nurse about an hour earlier. Bonita held his hands tightly, rousing him in the process, and he opened his eyes. A faint smile streamed across his face on seeing Bonita before he gradually dozed off again. Little did he realize that his life challenges had just jumped from the frying pan into the fire.

After his discharge from the hospital, Bonita explained to Kamal what happened between her and Kandie. She explained to him that "Halloween Kandie" was up to no good. Kamal was caught in the middle of a crisis between Bonita and Kandie. He wanted to be involved in the life of his only child. Trying to reach a compromise was impossible, as Bonita did not ever want to see Kandie again. In the end, Kamal settled for spending a few hours every month with his son away from home. This arrangement did not make Kamal happy at all, especially since Bonita was now pre-occupied with getting pregnant to have a child of her own.

As he closed his eyes to sleep after spending only four hours with his son earlier in the day Kamal reflected on his predicament saying to himself "What I have is a loving wife who does not have a child but makes me happy. I am happy even though I don't have what I don't have with her and I am happy with what I have with her. What I have is an ex-wife who controls my access to my only child. What I have is an ex-wife who is trying to seduce me to get me back. What I have is an ex-wife who is trying to ruin what I have that is making me happy right now."

However, things took a turn for the worse a couple of months later.

Should we pity the house or have sympathy for the tree?

Part Three: Section Two:
What I Want

When he was feeling much better and back to his full activities, Kamal raised issues with Kandie over the phone based on the report he got from Bonita. She blew it off, claiming that Bonita was exaggerating. She explained that she had switched Kamal's phone off so that he would not be disturbed and would recuperate in peace with little or no disturbance from people.

"So, why did you not inform Bonita that I was injured?" Kamal queried her.

"You told me that she had a family emergency and had to travel home to her parents. Did you think it was a great idea to then give her such bad news about you? Don't you think that it would be very inconsiderate on my part to do that to her?" Kandie asked him rhetorically.

"I get your point," Kamal acknowledged. "However, she said that she was looking for me everywhere?"

"I am sorry, but I did not realize that you would have wanted me to post it on the internet and report to CNN that you were injured."

"You know very well that that is not what I meant," Kamal countered.

"I don't know what you mean, but it sounds like you are blaming me for taking good care of you when your wife was away attending to another family emergency," Kandie retorted.

Kamal paused. He knew that Kandie indeed took care of him when he was injured, but he also felt that Kandie had a hidden agenda of her own. He did not want to sound ungrateful to Kandie, but at the same time, he did not want to fall into her trap.

"I am sorry," Kamal apologized. "Thank you for taking care of me when I was injured."

"No problem at all. I am very sure that you would have done the same for me. After all, the fact that we are not together now does not mean that we do not care about each other," Kandie replied.

Kamal did not know what to infer from Kandie's statement, but it rings true. After all, if Kandie were the one who was injured in his presence, he truly would have taken care of her too. Nevertheless, there was something about Kandie's statement that made Kamal uneasy. He just couldn't figure out what it was.

Nonetheless, Kamal reduced his visitation to his son and suspended the idea of Junior coming to spend the weekend with him and Bonita. He cited his health reasons even though it was purely to avoid upsetting Bonita who was still bitter about what Kandie did when Kamal was injured.

During one of Kamal's self-imposed limited visitation with his son a couple of months later, Junior asked his father if he could borrow a dollar from him. This caught Kamal by surprise, and he asked him what he wanted to do with a dollar. Kamal Junior explained that he wanted to buy a very good gift for his mother for Mother's Day. Kamal felt that this might be another mischief orchestrated by Kandie. However, he did not want to disappoint his son.

"So, why do you want to buy something for your mum?" Kamal asked his son.

"The television said to do something special for mummy on Mother's Day," he replied.

His response sounded innocent enough to Kamal. So, he agreed to take him to the nearby mall to get something nice for his mother. Kamal bought a Happy Mother's Day card, a box of chocolate and a bouquet of flowers. He gave these to Kandie as a gift from his son when she came to pick him up at the designated time in the park. Kandie thanked Kamal for his gesture. When she opened the card, a voice recording said "Happy Mother's Day. You are a great mum!" She then quickly read the content of the card.

<u>My lovely everyday mum</u>
For me, every day is Mother's Day
Not just on a Sunday in May

You have been my mother every day
You fed me every day
You cleaned me every day
You groomed me every day
I will always be grateful every day
Not just on a Sunday in May

You taught me every day
You watched over me every day
You showered me with love every day
You endured sleepless nights for many a day
I will always be thankful every day
Not just on a Sunday in May

Your cooking makes my day
Your smile refreshes like the breeze of the bay
You always stand by me in every way
You always encouraged me all the way
For me, Mother's Day will always be every day
Not just on a Sunday in May.

Thank you for all you've done for me.
I love you, mum.
Always have, always will.

Kandie hugged her son tight and said a heartfelt, *thank you, my dear,* as tears of joy rolled down her cheeks. She remembered the 'good old days' when Kamal used to write poems for her and showered her with gifts. She wished those days would come back. She wanted those days to come back.

She just had to figure out how to make it happen. As she held her son's right hand and led him towards her car, she looked back and saw that Kamal was still looking at her. She smiled at him and waved goodbye. Kamal waved back and headed for his car to drive home.

When Kamal got home, he found Bonita weeping. He was shocked. In between sobs, Bonita asked Kamal, "Did you tell Kandie to mock me?"

"What are you talking about? Why on earth would I do that?" Kamal asked in a loud tone.

"Leave me alone," Bonita responded as she walked towards the bedroom.

Kamal followed her and held her left shoulder. "Honey, I am sorry, but I really don't know what you are talking about."

Bonita took out her phone and showed Kamal the text message she received from Kandie.

It read, "To all mothers out there, Happy Mother's Day. I just got these wonderful presents from my son." She also attached the pictures of the bouquet of red roses, the exquisite chocolate pack and the beautiful card signed Kamal Junior.

Kamal was dumbfounded. "Why did Kandie behave like this?" he asked himself. "Why did she decide to send this text message to Bonita knowing fully well that she doesn't have a child? What is she trying to achieve?" He asked himself. Even though the content of the text message seemed harmless but sending it to Bonita would surely provoke a negative feeling. Kandie should know better than that. He felt like calling Kandie immediately to rebuke her, but he realized that it was much more important to console Bonita. Fighting Kandie can wait.

"Honey, I am so sorry," Kamal apologized to Bonita. "I did not expect her to do that."

"But you bought those gifts for her..." Bonita affirmed.

"Yes, I did. But it was because Junior wanted to buy a special Mother's Day gift for his mum," Kamal tried to explain.

Bonita shook her head and remarked, "I guess mothers

are more special," in a very sad tone and she burst into tears.

Hearing this made Kamal very sad too. He hugged Bonita and remarked, "You are very special my love. I am sure that you will be a wonderful mother."

"When?" Bonita asked Kamal.

Kamal had no immediate answer to this deep emotional question. "Very soon my dear, very soon," he finally mumbled.

Kamal remained in a pensive mood throughout the night. He could not sleep. He held Bonita's hands to reassure her that he is there for her. He wondered why some women always hurt other women in this regard. Is it deliberate to show that they have something that others do not have? Is it inadvertent that they are not thinking of the sadness they bring to others when they tout the fact that they are mothers? Yes, it is true that mothers suffer and sacrifice a lot for their children. However, it is no excuse for them to make those who do not have children feel sad in their plight. Calling a spade, a spade, it is not that those who are blessed with children did something special or exhibited special skills that got them pregnant in the first place. Kamal noted to himself that some mothers did not even want the children when they had them. A good example is Kandie herself who is now deliberately making Bonita sad. Kamal recalled that Kandie did not want to have a child at that time and she even threatened to abort her pregnancy. He echoed the faint call in the society that "every day is Mother's Day." He truly believes it. Just like the card he bought for Kandie stated, he is convinced that children should be thankful to their mothers every day not just on the second Sunday in May. However, there is no justification for making other people sad while celebrating what you have.

As he was finally dozing off, his mind wandered about Father's Day, which he quickly dismissed. There is no such thing as a real Father's Day celebration in this society, he noted. Unlike Mother's Day, when mothers are treated well and showered with affection and nice gifts, most people don't even know that there is something called Father's Day. For those who do and make attempts to make daddy feel special, their approach is too symbolic and sometimes too half-witted. If they buy him a tie, it is because they want him to hang himself with it. If they buy him socks, they are merely telling him what they think of him. Disturbingly, those are actually the lucky fathers. Others don't get anything on Father's Day, or they get something which the ladies will use, but it will be first presented to the father. He recalled talking to a senior colleague, Mr. Daniel, at work a few years previously. When the issue of Father's Day came up, Mr. Daniel had told him that when he had complained of not getting anything for Father's Day, his wife went to the supermarket, bought a blender and presented it to him as his Father's Day present. A few minutes later, she came to take the blender and informed him that the blender in the kitchen had broken down. He remembered how they all laughed. Mr. Daniel then told them that the following year, his family decided to take him out to dinner for Father's Day in an exquisite restaurant in Washington DC. The meal was fantastic. He really enjoyed himself until the waiter brought the bill. Everybody stared at him in expectation for him to pay for the meal with his credit card. Poor guy! He had no choice. He had to pay for the meal. Poor Mr. Daniel. Poor men. Poor fathers of the world.

When Kamal finally saw Kandie in person, he thought of rebuking her for what she did with the Mother's Day gift, but four weeks had passed since the event, so he just let it slide, promising himself never to let it happen again.

Four days later, Kamal was at home while Bonita went out for some domestic chores. He heard a knock on the door. It was the delivery guy for the United Parcel Service (UPS). The UPS guy asked Kamal to sign for a beautifully wrapped package from someone named Ya Truelove. He signed for it but was puzzled because he did not know anybody by that name. When he opened it, he found a Giorgio Armani suit that was his perfect size with a note that read "Happy Father's Day from Kamal Junior."

Kamal was stunned. He did not know what to do. Should he tell Bonita? Should he reject a Father's Day gift from his son? He quickly corrected himself that the suit was actually from Kandie. After all, his son does not have any money to buy an expensive suit. Is he supposed to accept this very expensive gift from Kandie? He tried to rationalize that he should take the suit. After all, he is paying spousal support to Kandie without getting any benefit from her. The thought quickly switched into anxiety when he heard Bonita's car pulling into the driveway.

> **Author's note:** What should Kamal do? Should he accept the gift and pretend that nothing happened?

Kamal looked at the suit again. It was really nice. Kandie must have spent a fortune on it. It then dawned on him that returning the suit may damage the relationship between him and Kandie and his son. On the other hand, keeping the suit can damage the relationship between him and Bonita. He was not sure what to do. However, what is the use of having a nice expensive suit that he dared not wear, could not give away, nor return to Kandie who bought it for him? As the doorknob turned, he quickly removed the "From Ya Truelove" from the package, tore it and put it in his pocket having fully understood it meant, "From Your True Love." He left everything else on the dining table so that Bonita could see it and they could discuss it.

After Bonita saw the gift, she was emotional and had mixed feelings. She wanted to tell Kamal straight away not to accept the gift but send it back immediately to Kandie. However, a part of her also cautioned her not to let her anger negatively affect her husband and would then drive him into Kandie's arms out of sympathy. She knows that Kandie is a very conniving woman who appears to be bent on ruining her marriage to Kamal so that she can have a second chance with him. This must be prevented at all costs. She also could see clearly that her husband is very sincere in his dealings with her and really cares about her, but Junior is his son, and there is no denying that fact. In the end, Bonita sighed and remarked, "I don't know what to tell you."

Kamal held Bonita's hands and remarked. "You are the

joy of my life. Your happiness is my joy. Please, don't stop being who you are."

Joy
When you enter a room
It becomes alive with light
When you enter a garden
Even the flowers become brighter

When you are in the presence of peacocks
They become overwhelmed with humility
When you stand in front of chameleons
They become radiant with beautiful colors

When you came into my life
You brought a sweetness I have never tasted before
And I developed a feeling that I have never had before

When I asked you to be my wife
I was happy, I couldn't ask for more
For you are the joy I never had before

I love you

Bonita hugged Kamal and started crying on Kamal's shoulders while he fought his tears. He hugged her tightly, trying desperately to reassure her that all would be fine. Kamal packed the suit back into the delivery package and left it on the dining table. He was still confused about what to do with it. One thing is certain though; he is not about to wear it.

The emotional challenge
The lady who is kind to me
Has her challenges
The lady who is mean to me
Has her challenges

I am enjoying kindness
On the one hand

I am enduring meanness
On the other hand

What do I need to do
To repay her kindness?
What do I need to do
To mitigate her meanness?

As the dark clouds heralded the coming of the night with the croaking sounds of frogs in the nearby ponds while crickets made people aware of their presence by sound but not by sight, Kamal reflected on his life and his predicament. "What I want is for my loving wife to remain happy whether we have a child or not. What I want is my ex-wife to let me have access to my only child. What I want is for my ex-wife to leave me alone and go find herself another husband."

Part Three: Section Three:
What I Need

Kamal opened his eyes, but he did not feel refreshed. He turned and looked at his watch, the time read 1:35 a.m. He thought there must have been a mistake. He looked at the clock on the table. To his utmost surprise, it also read 1:35 am. The reality dawned on him. He had only fallen asleep for less than 45 minutes. He has been very anxious. That day, the Friday before Father's Day was going to be a special day. It was going to be the dawn of a new day of hope. The hope of a new beginning. The beginning of the preparation for the journey into motherhood for Bonita and parenthood for both of them. His mind started racing again in anxiety, wondering what opportunity laid ahead for him and his beloved wife. Would she be a good candidate? Would it work? Would they be able to afford it? How would it turn out? Any side effects? Is there any stigma involved? Yes, they have heard a lot about fertility enhancement and in vitro fertilization, but this felt very personal. This is a situation without guarantees. He then cautioned himself, that at least, they will have the opportunity to ask questions when they meet Dr. Childlove later that morning, precisely at nine a.m. He looked at his watch again. They only had 6 hours and 49 minutes before the appointment time. Kamal tried desperately to convince himself to try and get some sleep. He closed his eyes, but opened them only five minutes later. He looked at Bonita. She was fast asleep. This made him a bit happy. Well, his wife is getting a much-needed rest. Looking at her pretty face made Kamal smile. *Bonita is really pretty*, he mused to himself. He was amazed that despite how unhappy Bonita was in terms of all the problems that Kandie had been giving them as a couple while trying to ruin their marriage, she was still holding things together. Wow! *She is really pretty*, he said to himself again and chuckled. That thought made him happy.

On their way to the fertility clinic, Kamal held Bonita's left hand with his right hand while driving with only his left hand, "We will be okay. Everything will be alright," he said to his wife in an attempt to reassure her. He tried to appear confident even though he was very anxious. He just felt that it was his duty to appear calm and confident. Today is not a day to show any weakness, emotional frailty, or doubt. Definitely not today. They held each other's hands while sitting in the waiting room. There were many magazines in the center of the table, covering social issues, health, leisure, sports, and fitness. The television seemed to be showing only health-related programs.

After both of them completed the intake forms, signed essential privacy documents and took care of the 'all-important' payment information, they had their vital signs taken with measurements of their blood pressures, temperatures, pulse, respiratory rate, height, and weight.

After another fifteen minutes of waiting, they were both ushered into a private consultation room to await their consultations with Dr. Childlove, who came in approximately five minutes later. Dr. Childlove looked a lot older than his picture on the website. Well, it only reflected that he has experience. "At least, maturity translates into experience in medicine. Furthermore, this was not a dating service of online to offline to in-person dating, or whatever they call it these days when pictures are modified deliberately," Kamal said to himself. The clinic probably forgot to upload a more recent photograph. His wandering thoughts were cut abruptly when Dr. Childlove introduced himself and extended his hand for a handshake with Kamal. He had a strong handshake which to the former soldier in Kamal meant confidence.

Kamal turned to Ray, "We have been trying for three years to have a child, but we did not seek any extra help because we had each other, and we were quite content with the belief that children would come when they want to come. We had a couple of false alarms in which her period was delayed for a few days, and we would be hoping that we hit the jackpot only for the hopes to be dashed a few days later. However, all these problems from Kandie made Bonita so unhappy that we agreed to try the scientific conception method. This can really be tough. Think about somebody who has always pride herself in natural products only, nothing artificial, organic vegetable, free-range hens laying natural antibiotic-free eggs, eating free-range chicken and turkey, wild-caught fish, et cetera, now to have to resort to scientific methods to assist in conception. It felt like using fertilizers and chemical weed killers. Having to take hormones to increase egg production felt like using high dose fertilizers, and in vitro fertilization is like genetically modified foods. However, the natural love one has for children makes you overcome your objections because you dub having children as a necessity just like adding chlorine to water or fluoride to public water to prevent tooth decay among children. Sometimes, circumstance makes us do what needs to be done."

"Bonita went to her primary care physician who checked her for thyroid problems, diabetes, and every disease on the planet. All the tests were normal. She had never been pregnant. My soldiers were examined too to ensure that they were strong in number and stamina. This is necessary in order to ensure that my legacy explorers can get to the promised land to conquer and not be conquered. I must say that I was happy to know that my warriors were combat-ready in millions, even though only one soldier is needed to raise the flag and plant his sword on the ground for posterity. Later, her primary care physician recommended that we should see a fertility doctor given her age of 33. Time was of the essence. The truth is that those who are blessed with children effortlessly cannot fully appreciate what those who have to deal with infertility go through."

Ray and Adam nodded in agreement.

Kamal looked at Ray and commented, "Intimacy for the sole purpose of procreating as soon as possible is no fun at all. We started having intimacy by the clock and by parameters that suggested the ovulation period. Our dancing to the silent drums became intimacy without intimate moments, just mechanical. Intimacy became work rather than relaxation, anxiety rather than comfort. Every period became a challenging period. Every period brought sadness to my darling," Kamal lamented.

"That will be in total contrast to Desiree," Ray noted. She was always ecstatic whenever she sees her period.

"She was always happy that she was not pregnant?" Adam inquired.

"No, she was happy that I would not be asking for her treasures, and she is naturally free from me with a perfect excuse to leave her alone until her period is over. Unfortunately, when her period is over, she will still return to actively chasing me away and denying me my right."

Period

It is the irony of life, period.
It is a special period, period.
It is a challenging period, period.
It is a painful period, period.

No period is ordinary, period.
There is no ordinary period, period.
Her period is a valid excuse, period.
Her period is an escape, period.

Although she is losing something, period.
But not being bothered by him, period
Is the best part during that period, period.
Hmmm. What a period, period!

With every period, period.
Somebody is losing something, period
and somebody is not gaining anything, Period.
Hmmm. What a period, period!

"During the consultation, we got a lot of information from Dr. Childlove, he answered our questions and allayed our fears even though there was no guarantee. In vitro fertilization costs about $15,000 out of pocket, but he explained to us and encouraged us to get some tests done through our primary care physicians which our medical insurance will cover."

When Kamal and Bonita got home later in the afternoon, they relaxed on the sofa in the living room since both of them took the day off from work to attend to their family health needs. The mood of Bonita had gone from sad and gloomy to enthusiastic and hopeful after their consultation with Dr. Childlove. Although she was happier about the prospects of having a child of her own, the behavior of Kandie towards her continued to echo in her mind. Suddenly, she chuckled spontaneously without any stimulation of sight or sound from anybody, and whispered, *Thanks, mum.* Although she did not intend for Kamal to hear her, he did. Kamal had noticed the increased happiness in Bonita's demeanor while she was counting the fingers of her right hand and observed that she was smiling from 'Cape to Cairo' before she made the 'thanks mum' remark.

"It sure feels great to see you very happy," Kamal remarked. "What were you thinking of just now that gave you a boost of happiness?"

"I remembered a piece of advice from mum," Bonita replied.
"What did she say?" Kamal inquired being very curious.
"She told me to take very good care of you and my home. She said that more often, people think that the husband is the

one who takes care of the wife, but the reality is that it is actually the wife who looks out for the husband and protects his interest," Bonita responded.

"I knew it!" Kamal exclaimed.

"Knew what?" Bonita asked him.

"I have always known that your mother loved me more than she loved you," Kamal replied.

"Yeah, yeah, yeah. Whatever. However, I am going to make you a deal," Bonita expressed to Adam with seriousness in her voice.

"What deal?" Kamal asked his wife wondering what she meant.

"I am going to give you to a Father's Day treat on my terms and conditions," Bonita responded, smiling.

Kamal lifted his head from Bonita's right thigh and sat up with a very curious look on his face.

"Okay. What are the terms and conditions?" Kamal asked her.

"I am going to treat you to an early dinner on Father's Day in a restaurant of my choice."

"That's fine," Kamal interjected.

"And you will be wearing the Giorgio Armani suit," Bonita explained.

"What? You can't be serious!" Kamal replied, being very surprised.

"I am very serious. That is why it is on my terms and conditions. Moreover, it is a very nice suit, and it is yours."

Kamal was not sure what to make out of the turn of events. He could not fathom why Bonita would want him to wear a suit that she knew was from Kandie, whose sole purpose was to sow discord between them. However, if that is what Bonita wanted, then he would go along with it to make her happy.

"I must say that I am surprised about your insisting that I wear the suit, but it is your call. Well, as you said, it is on your 'terms and conditions,' and there is nothing I can do about it." Kamal made air quotes while saying 'terms and conditions.'

On Sunday afternoon at four p.m., it was time for the couple to go for the early dinner treat that Bonita promised her husband in celebration of Father's Day. Kamal was formally dressed as required by Bonita. He wore his Giorgio Armani suit with a matching necktie and highly shinning plain toe Oxford dress shoes. Bonita wore a light red traditional maxi dress with ruffle detail adorned with pink embroidered flowers. Her wrists ornaments were with two three-piece sets of 18 karat gold bangle bracelets. The round diamond halo pendant necklace gave her a sophisticated look, and she completed her dressing with a Mexican hat embellished with woven band and beads. Kamal looked at his wife and remarked, "You look absolutely stunning. If not for the fact that this is being done on your terms and conditions, I would have opted for us staying at home for me to continue staring at you and remain transfixed in my semi-consciousness while relishing in how lucky I am to have you."

Bonita smiled in appreciation and threw herself in her husband's arms, and they shared a passionate kiss. Bonita then suggested that they take multiple pictures in singles and selfies together. Subsequently, they left for Faazee Pollo and Steak Grill on Eastern Avenue. Bonita politely asked the gentleman in charge of valet parking to kindly take their pictures. Bonita and Kamal took several pictures in several affectionate poses using Bonita's smartphone. Bonita looked at the pictures and remarked, "Perfect!" She then gave a generous tip to the valet parking attendant before he got into Kamal's car to drive it away for parking. The dinner was fantastic. Kamal was very appreciative of Bonita's gesture, and they capped the Father's Day celebration with a perfect night. As Kamal was transitioning to dreamland, he said to himself, what I need is a wonderful wife who loves and cares about me. What I need is a baby with my loving wife so that she can be happy. What I need is for my ex-wife to absolutely leave me and my wife alone.

<u>With and without you</u>

I am somebody on my own
But I will be nobody without you
I am something on my own
But I will be nothing without you
I am here on my own
But I will be nowhere without you
I am in my time on my own
But my life will be boring without you
Because time is better spent with you

The fact is that you compliment me
The truth is that you complete me and
The reality is that you perfect me

Thank you for being with me
Thank you for being here with me
Thank you for being there for me

I love you

Epilogue

Kandie looked at her phone for the umpteenth time—no messages. "Today is Sunday, Father's Day, and it is already 10:15 pm," she mumbled to herself. She was convinced that she would get a call from Kamal two days ago on Friday but did not receive any message. On Saturday, she was certain that she would get a call or at least, a text message from Kamal but she did not receive any message. Kamal junior was already asleep. "Today is Sunday, Father's Day, and it is now 10:25 pm," Kandie spoke to herself loudly unable to hide her frustration. She was sure that the suit was delivered to Kamal three days ago. She expected him to call and thank her for the gift or at least thank his son for the gift. She had confirmed the delivery by UPS. Nonetheless, she decided to recheck. She logged back on to her computer and accessed the tracking information on UPS website, and it had the delivery confirmation that Kamal signed for the package on Thursday as planned. Definitely, he has the suit, but it is much unlike Kamal not to be appreciative, Kandie reminded herself. However, she was restraining herself from calling him, for fear that Bonita may be with him and she wouldn't want her call to be something that would then bring them together, just in case her strategy is working, and both of them are fighting at that time.

Kandie recalled the skirmish in the hospital with Bonita and how she was shamefully escorted out of the hospital by the security guards after Bonita produced her husband's divorce papers and her official marriage certificate, establishing that she is the real wife of Kamal at the hospital. Kandie felt a bitter taste in her mouth as she put her phone down on the kitchen granite counter-top. Kandie decided to go to the bathroom. As she was about to open the bathroom door, suddenly she heard her phone made a sound of receipt of a text message. Kandie quickly turned back to pick her phone. She was excited to read the content of the message and quickly drew a pattern on her smartphone to unlock it so that she could read her message. Then she got another text message. Kandie was shocked that the two messages were from the same person, the last person on earth she wanted to hear from—Bonita. Kandie was disappointed that the message was not from Kamal, but she was doubly disappointed that she had turned back from the bathroom to receive text messages from Bonita. As she opened the first message, she realized it was a picture of Bonita and Kamal together in a passionate embrace with Kamal's car in the background. Kandie's hair stood on edge as she realized that Kamal was wearing the Giorgio Armani suit. Then Kandie received more pictures and text messages from Bonita. The first message read "Kandie, Thank you very much for the suit. It was a perfect fit, he looked so hot in it, and I gave him all my love." The second picture had Bonita sitting across on Kamal's legs while he looked adoringly at her. The accompanying text message simply stated, "With all my love." The next five pictures also had Bonita and Kamal in varying romantic postures with Kamal wearing the Giorgio Armani suit. One of the pictures had "Happy Father's Day" in the background. It was the picture that Kandie hated the most because Bonita was putting some food in Kamal's mouth in it. The accompanying text message said, "Tastes so good - feels so good - like it should." Kandie dropped her phone on reading that text message, and the screen of her smartphone cracked when it hit the floor. This increased the anger of Kandie by a thousandfold. Bonita sent Kandie eight pictures, and she hated them all. Kandie thought of blocking Bonita's number so as not to receive any more irritating pictures and text messages from her. Her urge to use the bathroom disappeared. Surely, things had not turned out the way she had planned. She did not consider the possibility that Bonita and Kamal could be on good terms after he got the suit, enough for him to actually wear it. "I did not see this coming at all," Kandie said to herself with regrets. "The possibilities I had considered were:

1. Kamal does not inform Bonita, but Bonita sees the suit and confronts Kamal. He tells her the truth that he did not encourage me to do it. However, like most women, I expect Bonita not to believe her husband. I mean, every woman knows to be

suspicious of her husband when it comes to the issues of ex-lovers since we believe that men will always have nostalgia for the past. I expect them to end up fighting and thereby, create a crack in their marriage that can slowly widen until I am able to penetrate it more and be able to get my man back.

2. Kamal does not inform Bonita and pretends that he bought the suit himself. This is my preferred scenario. That way, I will have leverage over Kamal also. I have the receipt of purchase, the delivery charges, and all documentation regarding the suit. I can use it to blackmail Kamal into submission in the future, especially if he keeps resisting my love advances. I can also send the information to Bonita in the future to convince her that she had overstayed her welcome. She should leave us alone since Kamal and I are back together, and my family has been reunited. After all, I am the one Kamal truly wanted. It was the little challenge we had that opened a small window for Bonita. We are ready to close the window now. Bonita should go away.

3. Kamal informs Bonita himself, but she picks a fight with him because she does not believe him that he did not encourage me. This will make Kamal very angry because he knew he told her the truth. So, he starts resenting Bonita too. This will eventually give me a much-needed break to create a wedge between the couple. They were not supposed to be together anyway. It was supposed to be Kandie and Kamal only. End of story.

4. Kamal informs Bonita, and she insisted on him returning the suit. I will then pick a fight with Kamal and prevent him from seeing his son. I will do everything possible to frustrate his efforts and thwart his attempts to see his son. In any case, I will not take the suit back from him. I will constantly prick his conscience by saying, "You can go and throw away the gift from your only child if you want." I will keep reminding him that

he is not appreciative of my sacrifice for him and accuse him of not caring about the emotional well-being of his son. After all, technically, it was his son who got him the suit as a Father's Day present. I will do this until he starts feeling sympathy for my son and me."

However, she did not play or think of a scenario in which Kamal accepts the gift, and Bonita still loves her husband. Well, there has to be a way to end this madness. "It is on baby, it is on," Kandie promised herself, trying to overcome the unforeseen setback in her grand plan. "If I cannot succeed in separating Bonita from Kamal by myself, then it is time for *Operation Cold ICE,*" Kandie mused to herself as she typed in the Department of Homeland Security on Google search on her laptop computer. "We will see how long you can be giving him that stupid love of yours. This woman and her family need to go back to wherever they came from." She looked at the cracked screen of her smartphone and angrily sent a reply of, "We'll see," to Bonita.

Bonita looked at the response from Kandie and remarked, "Gotcha!' She smiled in appreciation of her mum's advice before her marriage. Bonita recalled that about a week before her marriage, her mum had 'taken her to school' by teaching her some words of wisdom regarding her marriage. Every day for five days, her mum held one finger of her right hand and told her about different challenges that may occur in married life and suggested possible solutions to them. Her mother literarily wanted her to know them, understand them, memorize them, and be able to apply them. That was why she limited her to one per day. On the sixth day, she summarized all five pieces of advice again, and on the eve of her wedding, her mum had insisted that she had to "regurgitate" the advice to her mum. She felt that she was being disturbed at that time, but now she appreciated what her mum did for her. That was why she was silently saying "thanks, mum" when Kamal heard her. Bonita started recalling the advice again to relish in her memory of the wonderful advice from her caring mother.

Bonita held her pinky finger and said, "**Number one**: Respect and take good care of your husband if you don't want others to take care of him for you."

She then held her ring finger and said, "**Number two**: Protect your husband's interest because you are his last line of defense."

She subsequently held her middle finger and said, "**Number three**: Never fight your husband because somebody else wanted you to do so." Bonita smiled, as this was the principle that applied to Kandie's failed strategy.

She then held her index finger and said, "**Number four**: Never fight your husband when he is having other challenges because he will not feel safe anywhere. However, if he feels safe with you, he will feel strong to confront challenges everywhere."

She then held her thumb and said, "**Number five**: Have a low threshold for happiness for yourself, and this starts with being content with little."

It was strange to her back then and still feels strange now, a few years later, that her part in the five pieces of advice was the lowly crooked thumb that looks different from the other fingers. Her mum had countered her argument then by telling her that the thumb may be funny looking, short, crooked, and away from the others, but it is still the most important finger. It gives strength to all the other fingers, and its presence and its strength is really the power and strength of the grip of that hand. It is the finger that will be missed the most if it is lost. Such is the parable and irony of a woman being happy in her marriage. She needs to find joy and happiness in her marriage, and to be content with little is the foundation for happiness for a smart woman.

Bonita then remembered that her mum asked her father to advise her on the eve of her wedding. He remarked, "I absolutely agree with your mum. In addition, I will tell you this; there are bound to be those moments of annoyance between you and your husband because both of you are not perfect. So, my advice is that you should never make any decision when you are angry because it will most likely be the wrong decision."

Bonita left the kitchen from where she had sent the pictures and text messages to Kandie. She went back to bed. Her husband remained fast asleep, totally oblivious of what had happened between Bonita and Kandie.

> **Author's note:** Do you agree with Bonita fighting back this way? Do you think Bonita should have discussed with Kamal before taking this step? Please indicate whether you are a man or woman when you respond to this question. Thanks.

Nora was tossing and turning on her bed in her pajamas. The clock on her dresser read 9:07 a.m. She looked up at the cathedral ceiling in her room, beautifully adorned with a decorative ceiling fan. The blades were not moving. They were at a standstill. "Just like my life," Nora remarked to herself. A part of her wished that she was asleep and was merely having a terrifying nightmare. After all, no matter how terrifying a nightmare is, what happens in dreamland stays in dreamland. However, this was no dream at all. It was a reality for which she had not prepared. "I know that many people will think that this is an easy decision, but they are wrong," Nora said to herself as she covered her face with the second pillow on her bed. "Why is the universe making things difficult?" she queried. If only Adam had been the rich young guy, the decision would be so easy. Her head would be in the clouds right now. If Richard had been the old guy with baggage, the rejection would have been swift, a total no-brainer. Everything is confusing or out of place. "Mummy is pushing for Richard, but I am not so sure if it is really for herself or for me, or for Richard's mum who happened to be her friend in college. Unfortunately, Daddy seems to be on the fence. I am sure of the love and care of Adam. Yes, he is old and not rich, but he truly loves me and really cares about me. Richard, on the other hand, is too fast for me. Sure, he is rich and young, but is he really happy with himself?" Nora questioned.

Suddenly, her thought was interrupted by her mum's voice, "Nora! Nora!! Don't let your breakfast get too cold. Come and eat. You have a big day ahead of you."

Aneida looked out of the window. The rain had started falling as predicted by the weather forecast guy on cable TV Channel 29 news a few hours earlier. Her radio was on WHAT 99.9 FM and was playing old music of the legends. She started hearing the soft melodious noise produced by raindrops as her curtain danced violently to the turbulence of the winds. She had completely forgotten to close the living room windows. She quickly rushed to close the windows, and suddenly, there was a thunderclap. It was as if the flash and the noise of the thunder jolted her into reality and reminded her that Adam's seeming interest in her had been a flash in the pan. She wondered why she had been waiting in vain for his love. Yet, she has a dilemma. She definitely did not want to push Adam away, but how will she make him come to his senses that time is of the essence? "Should I be pro-active? Instead of waiting for him to propose, why don't I ask him directly?" Aneida asked herself.

Desiree was livid as she angrily hung up her phone. "What an insult! What a great affront! Why on earth will anybody call me a failure? An underachiever? A doormat? An incubator? A baby caddy?" The more Desiree recalled the insulting words that were used to describe her, the angrier she got. She was the valedictorian in her high school, was on the honor roll throughout college, and had the highest grade point average in her graduating class in Marketing. She graduated *summa cum laude* and won many prizes at graduation. She could never imagine why anybody will classify her as a shame to the society. Desiree's eyes were red, both from crying and from being incredibly angry. Even if she were to die now, she would never expect anybody ever to say that her only achievement was being married to Ray Marshall. All of this coming from somebody she regarded as her best friend was too much to bear.

Suddenly, Ray entered the house.

"Hi Baby, I am home," Ray sounded excited and moved closer to his wife for a welcome kiss.

Desiree backed off and remarked, "Don't baby me."

Ray looked puzzled and responded, "Am I missing something here? What did I do to you?"

"Leave me alone," Desiree replied.

"Is something bothering you? I mean, when I left home this morning, you were doing fine. You even gave me a goodbye kiss and wished me luck when I was leaving for my interview this morning. Now, I am back, and instead of you asking me what happened with the interview, I found you being incredibly mad at me."

Desiree did not reply to her husband. She turned her back and started walking away.

"Are you depressed?" Ray asked, being very concerned.

Desiree turned immediately with profound anger in her voice "Depressed? Depressed? What did you mean by depressed? Do I look depressed to you? Do I appear depressed to you? Do I act depressed to you? Are you now a shrink that you now know what depression means?" As she asked all these rhetorical questions, she kept increasing her voice and kept walking angrily towards Ray, who started backpedaling, wondering what was going on with his wife. The more she used the word 'depressed,' the more depressed she appeared and the more depressing the situation became.

You caused it
You are the one
Who is depressing me
You are the man
Who is suppressing me
You are the dude

Who is repressing me
You are the guy
Who is compressing me
You are the husband
Who is oppressing me

Stop distressing me
Stop stressing me
Stop messing with me
Stop transgressing against me

Ray could no longer hide his frustration and yelled, "Desiree! Why are you addressing me in this condescending manner?"

THE END OF BOOK 2

ABOUT THE AUTHOR

Dr. Adeyinka O. Laiyemo is an Associate Professor of Medicine. He is a gastroenterologist and practices medicine in the District of Columbia. However, his heart is in art. He has done a lot of literary work as a features writer for The Daily Champion in Nigeria in the nineties. His poems have been published in anthologies in the United States.

Adeyinka loves comedy, poetry, and enjoys traveling. He is currently working on the concluding episode three of the trilogy entitled: **"Three Guys Talking: The Romantic Tragedy"**

SPOILER ALERT

Please do not turn over this page if you do not want to have an idea about how these stories conclude in Three Guys Talking: The Romantic Tragedy.

Three Guys Talking:
The Romantic Tragedy

Desiree wanted to prove her friend wrong by going back to school and joining the workforce, but her family responsibilities are in the way. Should she get a live-in baby-sitter to help her with all her responsibilities?

Ray got a part-time job to teach *Law and Ethics* in a community college for the additional income his family needs but soon found out that office hours for professors can be unexpectedly quite challenging.

Bonita and Kamal go for in-Vitro Fertilization. It is unclear whether it will result in successful delivery of a baby. Meanwhile, Kandie alleged immigration violation and gave information to the Department of Homeland Security, Immigration and Customs Enforcement in an attempt to have Bonita and her family deported from the United States.

Adam got married. Nora got married. Aneida got married. Richard got married. Are they happy in their marriages? Only time will tell.

Made in the USA
Middletown, DE
28 March 2022

63289031R00130